FIB BER

A novel by

WALKER ZUPP

MONTAG

A Montag Press Book
www.montagpress.com
Montag Press
777 Morton Street, Unit B
San Francisco CA 94129 USA

Montag Press, the burning book with the hatchet cover, the skewed word mark and the portrayal of the long-suffering fireman mascot are trademarks of Montag Press.

Printed & Digitally Originated in the United States of America
10 9 8 7 6 5 4 3 2 1

"The oppressed at least concluded that evil cannot be cast out by good."

— *Aleksandr Solzhenitsyn*

For Dexter Smith

DAY ONE

"…You will never reform me!" shouted the prisoner next-door for the second time. A voice like that rang out every couple of minutes.

It was dark and cold in the prison.

A dim row of hydrogen lamps provided light.

The moss on the walls repulsed Dante Fibber but not as much as the sentiments of his fellow prisoners. He was a man of medium build with a short beard and an afro. He wore a bubbly green coat, an old pair of leather trousers, and boots with straps on the worn sides.

"You will never reform me!" heard Fibber for the tenth time. He smelled something putrid. Was it him?

It was five in the morning when the guards woke Fibber up. They wore tight-fitting uniforms that reddened their faces and greyish knee-length boots that protected them from all kinds of prisoners.

"Stand up! Blankets!" they ordered maliciously.

"But I don't have any blan—"

"Shut up!" They marched Fibber through hallways and then entered an office where they threw him on the ground and departed.

Sitting at his desk, Sergeant Rostropovich glared malignantly at the prisoner. He was wearing the same uniform but was riddled with awards and medals. Vacuum-packed into his costume, a lieutenant stood idly in the corner like a lamp.

On the wall, there was a photograph of the Prime Minister wearing noble robes and dangling ceremonial bling from every extremity.

Out of habit, Fibber saluted the picture. "Cigarette?" he requested.

Rostropovich looked at the lieutenant who produced a cigarette and stuck it between Fibber's lips.

"Geese?" asked Rostropovich as he watched the prisoner.

Deprived of sleep, Fibber lit the cigarette and inhaled. "Thank you."

"A single goose according to the report—" Rostropovich shifted through the stamped papers, his passing hands reeking of after-shave. "—from which you took that most sacred virginity."

"What?" Fibber coughed.

"Why do you wish to complicate things?"

"I was told that I was being arrested for drunk and disorderly?"

"Do you always assume the morality of your charges?" barked Rostropovich. "The reports of the ministry are never wrong. Do you take issue with what I have said?"

"I'm not quarrelling with you, Rostropovich."

"A devilish deed or five in the report."

"Can you read the language in which it's written?" asked Fibber.

Rostropovich re-ordered the papers into a regal folder and slapped the folder on the hardwood desk.

He stood up to inspect Fibber. "You are not against a piece of goose, are you...or shall I say a piece of geese?"

"It was just a party."

"Damn you, Dante Fibber, and the magazine you were celebrating."

"It was a party! Everybody has parties!"

"A farm?" said Rostropovich. "Is a farm so necessary these days?"

A baffled Fibber caught on. "Christ...good God... my uncle has made claims against me?"

"Your uncle makes no such accusations." Rostropovich slapped the cigarette out of Fibber's shapely lips. "A report is a report...the ministry is the ministry."

"You want bibliographies?" pleaded Fibber. "I'm a patriotic poet. What else is there?"

"Have you no shame? Have you no respect for the geese?"

"I did not touch the geese!" he sputtered, catching his breath. "I chased a goose because I was drunk. That is why I chased it."

"Did you know that two committees were set up to run diagnostics on this case?"

Pinching the bridge of his Romanesque aquiline nose Fibber feigned tears.

"The Committee for Collation and Research was set up six hours ago. And the Committee for Constabulary Standards was set up *four* hours ago," Rostropovich reported dutifully. "Do you know what they found?"

"What?" asked Fibber.

"They ran tests on the same utterance and discovered that it was uttered by a monster. The utterance was, 'Come back and taste the honey you goose-bastards,' which is what you said."

"I did not say that." Fibber fidgeted with his twisted ragged nails.

"You are a liar."

Moving to the mantlepiece Rostropovich inspected his trinkets: a glass eye that had once belonged to a famous general and a tooth torn from a playwright whom Rostropovich hated.

"As there is no law and order anymore you are a lucky man. The recruits I get come and go like the weather; and then with every passing year they become more like the bastards—more like you."

"Rostropovich…are you letting me go?"

"Legally, there appears to be nothing wrong with deflowering geese," Rostropovich replied unenthusiastically as he returned to his seat. "No one would even bat an eyelid if you banged a pigeon in the county court."

"Apart from the pigeon, sir," chattered the lieutenant.

"Apart from the pigeon," echoed Rostropovich. "You're a poet," he directed toward Fibber. "Why don't you recite a poem something for us?"

"I can't do it on command."

"Your cousin lives on Vashlevsky Prospect," stated Rostropovich with abject intimidation.

With a heavy heart, Fibber decided that he had a captive audience. "Fine, this poem is called The School Choir." Which he then recited,

The designated worshipping mainstay
Cavernous and somewhat calculating
I half-expected the Chaplain to chase
Women half-aged and toupees aged replace
Alas, he ne'er hovered over Sundays
When prodigies drunk still from Saturday
Night gargled caffeine in the Holy place
Every square inch had to be parlayed
In the choir stalls, rich youth at their worst
Gossiping of teat-touching in great haste
You could almost forget this was a church
Organist scowling, conductor dismayed
To God vulgar energies are relayed.

The nonchalant foot-tapping of choir
Members without a doubt are quite stunning
Brains adrift, at least their blood warms the church
Here belief-loss gained instigates research
The chirping of life outside needs no song
Nor the breeze's guard modeled desire
Distracted passion, verve like flaking birch
Is Man's dominion: their ceaseless running
Of God's tract worth not the master spear
Nor annalists bracing salt over mirch
As Westerners do so well out of fear

If the prodigies shalt boredom prolong
Trade Christians for Christ, make the singing
wrong.

"Stop," interrupted Rostropovich. His collar was excep-
tionally tight. "Have you written the worst poem ever?"

"What?"

"You have no talent. It would be corruptible if you did."

Forgetting the transformative power of his verse Fibber
replied, "You can't do better than getting published in Loam
Magazine."

"Is that your confession?" Rostropovich eyed the playwright's tooth on the mantlepiece. "You're worse than Cornwall."

"I paid my council tax last month."

"You're joking." Beating the table with his fist Rostropovich struck fear into Fibber and his lieutenant who was mill-
ing around.

"Are you Mary Magdalene?" asked the lieutenant.

"You're not kosher because you pay your taxes," instructed
Rostropovich. "What about those countries where tax is paid
but evil continues to be committed?"

"They starve to death and die from disease," replied
Fibber.

"They don't spend their days defiling geese!" He gave the
lieutenant a message with his eyes, after which the young
man grabbed Fibber's afro and pulled it like a flushing cord.

Fibber wriggled in pain until Rostropovich raised a hand
and the pulling relented.

"Who would start that sort of rumour?" hissed Fibber.

"The report says as much," said Rostropovich.

"But according to you, not everything written is sacred."

"Then, we understand each other. May God bless this country and damn your poetry." Rostropovich sent another message with his eyes and the lieutenant removed his sausage-like fingers from Fibber's afro. He then pulled an envelope out of his pocket and handed it to Fibber.

"How do you punish an artist?" proposed Rostropovich with a smile. "How does one do it effectively and cheaply? It does no good to remove their tools because they continue creating in their head. The subversive mind is equally pernicious when compared to the pernicious poem."

He nodded, which Fibber took as a signal to open the envelope. He found a letter inside which was signed with the ministerial seal:

To Whom It May Concern:

The Belgian Invasion, led by one Plum Lukum, is pending. The Tectum is staffed but requires an overseer. Given your publication history, you'd be an ideal candidate. Your work begins at once.

I, Dante Fibber, consent to perform the overseer position.

Signature:_____

For the Glory of England
Tudor Wells
Minister of Defence.

Grabbing the edge of the desk Fibber looked as though he would faint.

"Is this a mistake?"

"Please sign where marked." The tone of Rostropovich's voice belied the hundreds of people for whom he had provided this service.

"What for?"

"You are a civil servant now." Rostropovich smiled weakly.

Having noticed the letter was a copy, Fibber signed the paper and passed it back to the lieutenant who stamped the paper several times using red ink.

Fibber saw the government's book of banned publications: a damaged leather-bound volume of a thousand pages that sat on the mantlepiece alongside the glass eye and the tooth.

"Where is my *Othello*?" asked Fibber.

"You mean that toilet paper you entered with? Who cares?"

"May I take it with me?"

The grumpy Sergeant Rostropovich went to study the banned publications. He licked his finger, scrolled through pages, and read that *Much Ado About Nothing* had been banned on the basis of nihilism. He also noticed that *Timon of Athens* had been banned on the basis of it not being very good.

"You won't have time to read." He could find no mention of *Othello*. "You're a civil servant now. You better get used to the long nights."

"If it isn't banned, shouldn't I be allowed to take it?"

Huffing like a steam train, Rostropovich replaced the book of banned books and ordered his lieutenant to return the copy of *Othello* to its rightful owner.

"Thank you," said Fibber soberly.

"I cannot see the appeal," sneered Rostropovich. "He's meant to be a general, is he not?"

"Indeed, sir," barked the lieutenant, joining the conversation.

"The best damn general in the Venetian army?"

"Indeed, sir. The best of the best of the best, sir."

"But that faggot Shakespeare expects me to believe that Othello can't tell when he's been betrayed?"

"Indeed, sir. *Call me Ishmael.*"

"It's just ridiculous. The type of thing you see in western operas."

"Indeed, sir."

"Now, get out!"

"Yes, sir." The lieutenant made to leave but Rostropovich interjected, "No! Not you!" He glared at Fibber. "Take your Shakespeare filth and shuffle off."

Fibber was then accosted by two policemen who ushered him into the outdoors. In keeping with the many dreary police dramas produced by state television, one of them was tall and beautiful, and the other was tall and beautiful but with terrible teeth. Moving Fibber like a potted plant they placed him in the back of a rover—a large vehicle commonly used for travel—and together drove away from the police station.

Fibber smiled when the rover drove through the gates of the city into the wilderness. The policeman with the terrible teeth piloted the vehicle into the outer wastelands whose skies varied solely between the heavy darkness of ignorance and the great light of wisdom and television. A single road demarcated their one touch of civilization. Fibber grew worried as they finally went off-road and traversed the uneven ground, unsure of what he looking at through the window.

In the distance, a huge stone head had been erected on the landscape. It must have been a thousand feet high with a large bulkhead where the mouth should have been. The eyes were little more than decorative flourishes. The girth of the structure became apparent, the closer they got. It must have been a Biblical building whose enclosing boundary was a good several kilometres around and whose presence and entity smacked of the ancient Yahweh.

A mud-covered ramp, which looked like a dirty tongue, ran up to the bulkhead in the mouth, its iron gleaming dully in daylight. The tall and beautiful policeman and his equally handsome colleague with terrible teeth parked the rover below the bulkhead, deposited Fibber like a bowel movement of little renown, and drove away.

There Fibber waited, watching the rover become a tiny speck on the horizon.

Then the bulkhead yawned open and out walked a woman called Minister Jozlov. She was a heavy-set woman wearing governmental robes. Her lips were thin and her grey-green eyes peered over her fat cheeks. Her brown fishtail braid was covered by a ministerial wimple and she stared out dolefully from her vantage point in the bulkhead's mouth. She beckoned Fibber to enter the Tectum. And so, he walked inside where she gave him the 'grand tour,' explaining his duties as they went.

Inside the giant structure were four floors and the ceiling of each floor featured chains. From these chains people suspended their belongings—and it was a storage-based solution that was simultaneously medieval and modern; Catholic and Protestant; inspired and irresponsible.

The first floor was designed for peasants; the second for business owners; the third for doctors, lawyers, and aristocrats; and the fourth floor was currently being prepared for some kind of entertainment. Minister Jozlov was in negotiations with the Metaphysical Circus to use the space effectively, environmentally, and comically. Fibber was also shown the basement which contained a furnace. The workers there had unionized and were causing trouble.

"The current collective bargaining arrangement is all but temporary," said Minister Jozlov. "But this way, we won't have to suppress them using the normal channels."

Fibber thought her mistruth belied her innocence.

In a matter of hours, the Tectum would be brimming with people taking refuge from the Belgian invasion. The immensity of the coming operation was sure to be overwhelming and as a result, Jozlov abandoned Fibber just after finishing the tour to bring him up to speed.

Standing inside the bulkhead Fibber began to register hundreds of people who were flocking to the wasteland in search of refuge. Taking their names and tax returns, he classed them by floors according to wealth. He then assigned them their plots on the relevant floors. They weren't fools and they certainly weren't worthless. What was wrong with them?

*　　*　　*

On the clean streets, the parliamentary buildings blocked the sky.

Inside a secret meeting was taking place in one of the cabinet rooms. Except for Minister Jozlov who was at the Tectum, every minister was present.

Professor Okonkwo was a squat academic type with flat feet. He wore a nylon shirt, jacket, and trousers—and seemed himself to be made of nylon.

"The bomb is in place," he addressed the cabinet coolly. "I will show what happens when the bomb explodes. First, I require instant coffee."

The instant coffee was sent for and appreciated by ministers who drank only the finest ground coffee from arctic bean farms. Okonkwo thanked the plump secretary and poured granules into a cup fashioned from traditional blue China bowls. "I require, also, a kettle…"

The kettle was sent for and appreciated by ministers who had never boiled water. This, they decided, was going to be a tough day.

Okonkwo thanked the secretary and plugged the kettle in. The water boiled and Okonkwo poured the sizzling liquid over the granules in the China bowl cup.

First, an explosion of heat in the middle.

Then the perimeter erupted and flattened the entire surface. Specks floated off into the oblivion.

"It will cool over time." Professor Okonkwo nodded conspiratorially as he referred his beady eyes to the map of the wasteland on the ceiling. "That will be the only necessary evil."

*   *   *

Having registered the thousandth person, Fibber was exhausted and leaned onto the bulkhead. Rain trickled down the ramp and the horizon was obscured by black clouds. As if he had walked out of a painting, a man appeared in the distance. He had cropped black hair under a purple beret and irritable eyes squinted by the rainfall. His jacket was baggy and tasseled and moved like a poncho. Beneath the jacket, he wore a plastic chainmail backgrounded by a golden medallion hanging from his thick neck. As he moved through the uneven terrain his corduroy trousers flexed as they tucked into his grey wellington boots which crushed everything in their path. Within a few minutes, the man had squelched through the last of the mud and had planted his feet firmly at the base of the ramp. He stared through the rainfall at Fibber who gazed back at him.

When nothing was said, Fibber came forward. "Are you Malark?"

"Fyodorovich Alexandrovich. Fyodorovich Alexandrovich. Fyodorovich."

"What?"

The man touched himself in what appeared to be a sarcastic manner. "I guess I *am* Malark. But I wish to God I were somebody else, especially in this pigswill. Are you the current Overseer?"

"You are the first person to ask me that." Fibber squirmed in his boxer shorts. They insulted his memories of more comfortable briefs that had been worn during his unhappy childhood. "Did you, by any chance, bring scissors?"

"I've enjoyed your poetry in Loam Magazine," said Malark. "Shame about the font."

"That is strictly illegal," muttered Fibber.

"As opposed to loosely illegal? Would that also cover the goose?"

"That was never proven," complained Fibber, whose mind returned to the imaginary crime he had been accused of committing. "Whatever you've heard, I cannot vouch for your sources."

"You have me wrong. I am not judging you," replied Malark.

"Yes, you are!" Then he winced and added, "But that doesn't mean it's true."

"Don't worry, *Overseer*. I shoot art school and distinctions with the same arrow."

"Are you another artist?" *Was there no end to his torment?*

Insulted and bereaved of accreditation, Malark clattered up the ramp. "Have you been living and screwing under a rock where dim sprogs continue with their heritage of ignorance?"

Unmoved by the insult, Fibber waited.

"I can't believe that you've never seen my work. The commune and the commune's exploits are known from here to Timbuktu. I wager that *too* many people know of us!" He spread his legs on the ramp but he started slipping. Then he recovered and stood normally. "I *am* the Great Malark!"

None the wiser, Fibber bemoaned the rainfall.

"You must have heard of the South Valley Commune? Otherwise, you are absurd and I've nothing to say to the absurd."

"Good," said Fibber as the rain increased around him and the deluded artist.

Next moment Malark ventured up the ramp and tugged on Fibber's beard. "With this, I would wager that you're a devotee of some Marxist fairy tales."

Fibber pulled back. "What's the difference?"

The pattering of rain backgrounded Malark's clanging boots. "A normal fairy-tale starts with, *Once upon a time*." He paused and smiled. "A Marxist fairy-tale starts with, *One day there will be...*"

The joke was a minor solace from the crushing pain that Fibber felt—and whether it came as the result of his twisted boxer-shorts or the world itself was hard to estimate.

"If I am to work under you then my life shall be impossible," decreed Malark. "And why must everything always come back to you?"

"Were you arrested too?"

"Indeed, the boys and girls in blue paid me a visit." Malark harrumphed.

"Is that proof that greatness has its price?"

"It ought to be reduced." Malark spat into the mud. "I unveiled my latest and greatest exhibition last night: a synthesis of realism and expressionism which I pinned to the walls without frames. Men and women who were secretly invited regarded my paintings with wonder and admiration. I was on form and sang with the sirens."

"I see." The rainfall grazed Fibber's skin. "Can we go inside, please?"

"My show was risky despite the invite-only procedure," continued Malark, irregardless of the fact that his beret had begun to resemble a wet tissue. "There was little difference in the end because an agent pulled me aside and showed me her badge. A night in jail with no sketches to show for it. In the morning I was forced to sign this ludicrous letter. What a death it must be to be eaten away by a spree of civil service. My mother was a civil servant and then she died."

Fibber checked his register and everybody was accounted for. "We really should go inside."

"There is a new restaurant called Karma where everyone is served what they deserve. It's a shame they opened in the parliamentary district." Malark clattered halfway through the bulkhead. "I'll tell you if I see Plum Lukum on the horizon. I wouldn't mind having a word with her."

Fibber slapped his hands on Malark's shoulders. "Easy. You're drunk."

"Only rainwater." He smiled. "You look like a misogynist. It's peachy to think women belong in the kitchen. But that's where the knives are."

"The first floor," instructed Fibber demurely, "needs to be locked before we go upstairs."

Malark detached himself and moved inside away from the rain where he removed the beret and slapped it against his thigh. "Don't forget the great chain of being," he said. "God, angels, humans, animals, plants, and minerals. Judging by this place we're no higher than the copper they mine for bullets. I never go up staircases before I know what type of angels hang about at the top of them."

They squidged through the bulkhead when something rumbled behind them. A rover bounded off-shrub and then squeaked to a halt at the bottom of the ramp.

A woman wearing an emerald waistcoat and an ankle-length dress opened the door and forced her knee-length metal boots into the sludge. She had frizzy red hair and thin eyebrows which gave away her noble brow. In her right hand was the end of a piece of rope that led into the rover. She tugged the rope when she exited the rover and there was a dwarf tied to the other end. He had a small afro and expressive eyebrows. He wore a puffy red jacket with identically coloured trousers and black laced clogs on his feet. Following the dwarf were two children who looked malnourished. The boy wore a raincoat and nothing else and plopped his bare feet into the mud where he wiggled his toes. The girl wore a potato sack with holes cut out for her arms. Her blonde hair was long and dirty and vexed the back of her neck like an octopus.

Ignoring the pompous lunacy of the scene, Fibber told them to hurry up. Staring at Fibber as though he had missed his cue, Malark stifled a laugh.

"The Tectum will be closing soon," related Fibber.

"Closing sale," muttered Malark.

Kicking her children up the ramp, Agapov yanked her dwarf along. "This, indeed, is an act of mercy. Isn't that right, children?" She turned to the dwarf as though he would tell her what to say next. "Is it not true that those who carry swords but know when to sheath them shall inherit the earth? If the earth is in that stone head, Honza, then so be it." Distracting herself using Fibber she waved. "You there! Are you the new Overseer?"

Fibber re-entered the rain. "Yes. What is your name?"

"Marielle Agapov. Madam Agapov. These are children."

"I'm not going to argue with you there," muttered Fibber.

"I haven't named them," declared Agapov lightly. "I call the boy, One, and the girl, Two."

("One, two, three!" snapped Malark.)

"You haven't given them names?" asked Fibber. "They look almost eight."

"Must they, Overseer? One and Two takes the cake."

"And three," added the Overseer as he nodded at Honza. But within seconds he realized that he had made a fatal mistake.

"It would be impossible to underestimate you," replied the dwarf.

"Oh...oh...I'm sorry...I didn't—"

"I'm thirty-eight and I don't know who the fuck you are," replied the dwarf with steam practically jetting out of his ears.

Then blocking the dwarf from view, Agapov waved her arm in a flattering manner. "I always forget to introduce my slave," she said. "This is my jolly slave, Honza!"

Malark shook his head underestimating the hypocrisy of the world and Fibber observed the bizarre party with horror and fascination. "You're practically attached," he observed.

"It's an act of mercy to have a slave in these times of ours: an act of mercy and a merciful pleasure. He does the cleaning."

"Yea, the thinking too," muttered Honza.

Rubbing his muddy fingers together, Malark consulted his superior in a whisper. Fibber nodded and then went inside. The deputy overseer remained and then turned on the suspicious woman, her slave, and her nameless children.

"A madam must have a spouse," began Malark.

"Must she?" She nodded away the accusations and sucked her teeth. "You are the deputy?"

"A lady must and I be he—*villain!*" He recognized her from wanted-posters in the city: she had murdered her husband in cold blood using a pair of scissors. "You are the woman who culled her husband," accused Malark.

"I've never heard anything so ridiculous." As Agapov spoke Honza winced like a man who had misplaced his trombone on the express train to Cardiff.

"I accuse a person of murder and then they babble sweet nothings." Scratching his plastic chain mail, Malark laughed rudely. "But all too coherently in your case, Miss."

"I am married, you chauvinistic pen-pusher."

"You do not deny it!" Welcoming the rain with his arms he focused on Honza's expressive eyebrows and meditated on them. "You know that braving the invasion yourself is illegal. Is your spouse at home in a coma? Where is this speculative partner?"

The boy urinated in the mud and the girl smoked a cigarette. Fibber laughed as he watched from inside.

"You bask in your accusations as well as your crime!"

The veil of kindness was lifted from Agapov fiery hair. The incandescent woman said, "How dare you accuse me of this!"

"I welcome your belated outrage," replied Malark, clapping. "You waited patiently for his return and plotted your dastardly plan and then executed it."

"Yes, I did! I did it! I killed the bastard!"

Honza shrugged. "I told you it was a bad idea." The curious sensation of warm urine touched his feet and he stared at the boy who blinked dimly and isolated his genitals. "What the—get yourself together youngblood!"

Agapov became stern and demented and pushed Honza with her boot. "Will you clam up? Your mistress is talking!"

Blowing a foggy ring of discontent, Fibber laughed. "Deal with this Malark. I'll wait for you inside."

"Vices," muttered Malark as he shooed the children inside and clinked towards Agapov where he severed the rope that held Honza captive.

"Great googly-moogly," exclaimed Honza with joy in his eyes. "Thanks, blanco niño!"

"I'm not white. I'm Peruvian."

"I'm eggs over-easy," cheered Honza as he stretched his arms and faced his former owner. "Don't worry about me, Marielle—worry about that double-chin," added the ex-slave, after which he staggered up the ramp.

"Deputy," pleaded Agapov. "I can only assume that you want something from me?"

"There's an opera by Richard Strauss where Apollo falls in love with Daphne and then turns her into a laurel tree."

The temperature of her eyes changed immediately. "You are a little chauvinist and I am going to get you."

"I'm going to give you a push and make sure you're planted." He gave Agapov an almighty shove which sent her plummeting off the ramp and splatting into a pool of mud. Then he scuttled inside where he initiated the lock mechanism.

Agapov struggled to stand up and grabbed the edge of the ramp. "Don't leave me, you bastard!" She dragged herself onto the muddy ramp where her body squealed against the muddy steel. "Come back!" She touched the bulkhead when the locks twisted shut and she was left lying in the rain and weighing up her misfortunes. Her rover sank deeper into the mud and was unsalvageable. "I'll kill you!" The wind of increase scattered free twigs. It stopped raining and would snow soon and she would need shelter, food, and water. "The children will live." She squeaked down the ramp. "They weren't mine anyway…"

In her office, Minister Jozlov was losing her mind. The manager of the Metaphysical Circus, a crude man known simply as the Maestro, was refusing to leave. He wore a cotton trench coat around his pear-shaped body and a porkpie hat that covered the globe of his hairy comb-over. He had purple blubbery lips and a goatee prickled with crumbs from a packed lunch. "*Minister* Jozlov," he crooned with self-satisfaction, "has anyone told you how beautiful you are? The individuals who appointed you must have won your affections and thus they are lucky swine."

"Maestro, get to the point—if that is your real name," replied Jozlov, "before I turn you into soap."

"Minister…" Behind him, other members of the Metaphysical Circus ambled around. Dodging another drip from the algae-covered ceiling the Maestro recovered his balance. "We require the fourth floor to ourselves. The problem is that our circus tent is tremendous and requires a great deal of space."

"Why should I not fill that space with countless souls?" asked Jozlov. Closest to the minister's desk was the Strongman who enjoyed picking his nose and sighing impatiently. As tall as he was wide, the Strongman wore a pair of belted leather trousers and knee-length boots secured by vicious straps. He was completely bald with a wise and friendly face which contrasted his body.

"There must and shall be entertainment," said the Maestro. "The first step in creating consent and maintaining control is through distracting the masses. Otherwise, you risk open revolt. I don't have to tell you that."

"Then why are you?" Jozlov wiped condensation from her desk as the Chicken Boy inspected her feet. The Chicken

Boy was the star attraction of the Metaphysical Circus and had been a member ever since he had been a tiny chick. Despite his beak, he had the head of a boy and the body of a chicken. He clucked pensively and pecked at the minister's feet. She kicked back, giving him a shock.

"Don't you agree with me?" whined the Maestro.

"Entertainment we require and entertainment there shall be. But what you want, and what you're going to get, are two very different things." Stamping two pieces of paper she took a deep breath. "It's my duty to inform you that the Overseer is a poet and that his deputy is a visual artist. They shall determine the artistic order of your world: in other words, what entertains, and what does not." She surveyed the Chicken Boy and frowned suggestively.

"A director's plate should not be full," replied the Maestro.

"I'll be in charge of your diet," Minister Jozlov said as she watched the Bearded Lady admiring one of her embroidered ministerial robes on the side.

The Bearded Lady had recently transitioned to a man and was wearing combat-trousers under his ankle-length dress. He had a magnificent beard with braided elements plus a well-coiffed mountain of hair reaching up like that of an aristocrat.

Minister Jozlov stood up, snatched her ministerial robe back from the Bearded Lady, and returned to her desk. "It's best to start with small meals," she concluded.

The Maestro grumbled unsatisfactorily. "Your metaphors are wasted on me."

"The Overseer and his deputy shall determine what you do and give you jobs. In other words, you'll be helping them—not the other way round."

"Can Jesus come and kill?" whispered the Maestro.

"They would like to put on a production of *Othello*."

He reddened and said, "Any chance there was of love, on my part, is now dead."

Meanwhile, the Strongman watched the Chicken Boy as he wandered into the corridor, pecked a deck of cards that someone had left on the ground, and then stared around, confused.

"Little bounder," said the Strongman.

"I can't fathom why," interrupted Minister Jozlov. "The idea of some brilliant general who can't tell when he's being deceived. I just don't buy it."

Dusting off his intellectual hat, the Maestro kicked the desk. "I believe the term is 'suspension of disbelief'."

"Suspension of grey matter, more like. You can kindly disappear now."

Biting his tongue, the Maestro pushed his performers out of the cramped room, their arms and legs kicking and flailing like frogs on a honeymoon.

"Did you ask about the gym?" barked the Strongman.

"Just get to the fourth floor in one piece!" ordered the Maestro.

"What about rune-stones?" asked the Astrologer. The Astrologer read tarot-cards, gave fortunes, and tolerated insane clients. She was petite, donned a loud headdress, and wore a purple sash around her waist and flip-flops the colour of rice pudding. "I could do with some rune-stones," she repeated.

"Just go! Go!" yelled the Maestro as he forced them into the corridor. Turning briefly at the door he saluted the minister and shut the door behind him.

Examining the mess around her, Minister Jozlov sighed. There were clothes dangling everywhere and the roof dripped condensation and motivated mould in the secreted corners of the room. She listened carefully and caught an occasional cry from below, through the floorboards and insulation.

She shuddered and sniffed.

"Clairvoyants," she muttered.

Malark and Fibber exchanged worried looks after the bulkhead had shut and they turned around. The first floor was saturated with peasants chasing children and baskets containing possessions. The smarter peasants hanged belongings from the chains provided and it looked like an alien forest half-brightened by rows of hydrogen lamps, the chains rippling from expulsions of air from nearby peasants.

"Willow trees," said Fibber as he pushed through chains suspending bags of potatoes. He refused to condone the gout and malnutrition that surrounded him. He paused in front of a dying ex-entertainer with a tambourine rattling under his chin and then turned to Malark.

"Where is Madam Agapov?" asked Fibber.

"Goats and monkeys!" Malark ignored the question. "Look at these scumbags. I've never seen such an incredible bunch."

"They're as wealthy as we were." He shrugged through his thick green coat. "Maybe they use petrol as cologne." His deputy pushed him forward with his hand and said, "You think all poor people are similar. But they are not." Their boots harmonized on the floor. "Look inside affordable housing and you will find several species of peasant. Don't forget it's we, the artists, who stink up those places." He wiped his nose on a paint rag as they tread past the mounds of peasants young and old. "But good art is hard to make, therefore most artists are poor too."

An elderly woman wearing a necklace of badger bones was eating the remains of a roast chicken that had been handed around a group of about ten people. Powdering her tight lips with her greasy fingers she almost choked on a wishbone. Still, she smiled, moving her tongue around her gums, and managed to pull out the wishbone from the back of her throat. Snapping it in two she showed the others what she had done and giggled.

"What about the artists who succeed?" asked Fibber.

"No artist is truly successful. Nor would I wish success on every artist."

"What about the great ones?"

"Tramps who trade paintings for meals and get appreciated in hindsight." Catching a fly in his palm he flicked it into a child's eye and clattered under the orange light vomited by an overhanging hydrogen lamp. "When they get old and unproductive, they run out of haggling materials and starve cynically in cafés."

"There are artists who are successful in their lifetime," claimed Fibber.

"Never permanently." Malark stepped over a family of four, each one of them wearing a filthy habit and trading rocks with nude men painted onto them.

"Does permanence separate a great painter from a banker?" asked Fibber.

"Yes," said Malark.

A man wearing an ushanka and trousers with holes was trying to start a fire by rubbing potatoes together. He cursed himself as his calloused fingers clashed dryly against the rough skin of the potatoes and their periodic poisonous nodules.

Blowing his nose Malark readjusted his beret. "What makes you think bankers are great?"

"Look at this place," said Fibber. "I think the bankers have done well for themselves." Swinging from a chain by Fibber's head was a goose wrapped in silicon. "I'll have you know that that's a dead goose…"

"You damn writer-bastards. You're always thinking of money." Malark's plastic chain mail was starting to itch and he fiddled with the skin under his neck. "Why don't you write about *these* people? How about a state of organized play where all the players agree on the rules beforehand? Not one where a couple hundred rule books get handed out to sprogs—and the rest have to get used to being ignorant. That's what I think about bankers and their banking."

On the ground, an ancient man crawled on all fours. He wore a red toga that had been sewn from several abandoned bedsheets and pineapple-scented sandals. His head hovered below Malark's kneecaps and suddenly he bit into his ankle.

Screaming Malark grabbed his ankle and hopped around looking for the villain. "I'm so sorry," apologized the toothless old man. "I have dreams, you see?"

"What dreams are these?" asked Fibber. "Where are you from?"

Drawing his knees up to his hollow chest, the old man spoke coldly. "In the morning my children woke me up and we travelled fifty miles to this place. When I asked them why they bothered me they answered that we had to get away from Plum Lukum. I refuse to believe all that claptrap. Where are the armies when you need them?" He held his stomach and looked to Malark for reassurance. "Children are good for nothing if they wake you in the morning and drag you outside." Then he squeaked something like regret and counted the toes in his sandals. "What the hell are you standing there for? Why can't you leave me alone?"

Having soothed his ankle Malark frowned tiredly. "You know who I am?"

The old man raced his tongue along his gums. "Senti Pita!"

"Huh?"

Fibber was surveying a slaughtered pig suspended from chains. "He means Saint Peter," explained the Overseer.

"Senti Pita! Senti Pita!" The toga rustled as the old man cheered.

Malark whispered in Fibber's ear: "Looney."

"If you are not Senti Pita then I don't want to know. I don't have patience for anyone who isn't." He clapped his feet as though they were his hands. "This better be heaven— I shan't get involved if it's not the case!"

"How is that for a wise man?" said Fibber as he elbowed Malark.

"Short of three."

"Well...there's us two." He wiggled the ears of the dead pig. "We could have this chap?"

"Leave the dead in peace," lamented Malark. "Why do they look like people? They're too human to be pigs."

The man who owned the pig was four feet tall and had a pinched mouth. He wore buckled shoes, undergarments, and nothing else. He stormed up to Malark and jutted out his chin. "Toad!" he declared.

Malark rounded on him. "What?"

Knowing a fight when he saw one Fibber seized Malark and pressed ahead. "Will you excuse my deputy? He has been away from his paints for too long. You know what that means: he can't think straight when he has no fumes to suck." He pushed Malark ahead who wriggled and fought back to have his revenge. "He better suck the right fumes," warned the pig man.

Below them, a young boy drawing Mary Magdalene using chicken entrails looked up and frowned at them. He said loudly, "You're going to make me pee with all your fighting."

"I'm going into withdrawal myself," whispered Fibber as he and Malark escaped the potentially ensuing and fatal crowd. "I've no time to write. But I expect that's the point."

Behind them, the pig's owner crawled into a ball and clutched the shiny buckles on his shoes. "I thought pork would get me out of this mess," he moaned.

Fibber came to his senses and began formulating what was going on here.

Why was it the Tectum had the air of an experiment? Yet it was safe to say that any city was usually an experiment. The same could be said for a town and therefore that every collective was simply an appraisal of combined existence: people living under the people.

Next moment a urine-stained dress fluttered into Fibber's eyeline and caught him by surprise. Grabbing a plastic bag dangling on a chain Fibber returned to the pig's owner, pulled the bag over his head, and whispered sweet nothings. He clomped back to Malark who was moving a boy around on the floor using one of his boots. "Is this kid bothering you? Grease mankind with shit and he'll walk for miles. We ought to pummel this incredible bunch. If you give me the signal, I will make tents out of their charity shop rags."

Fibber, cursing, clocked ahead and said, "Everyone is dry."

The boy slid under the chassis of a wagon and bonked his head as Malark put his hands on his hips. Then he turned to Fibber and said, "Where do you think you're going?"

"To work," replied Fibber as he avoided slipping on a patch of vomit.

"We are *in* our work." Beneath the violent glow of a hydrogen lamp, Malark smiled and paraded his motley collection of browning teeth. "We're in this damn head. I can't imagine people care about whatever work we get up to…" A wagon carrying barrels creaked out of the darkness ahead of them. It was pushed by a woman wearing a snood whose daughter stood waist-deep in pistachios in one of the timber barrels.

Meanwhile, Fibber tripped on another naked man. But this man subsequently looked at the Overseer, clapped his hands, and pointed at him for much longer than he needed to.

"God knows what that means," thought Fibber.

Turning his attention to the oncoming wagon, however, Fibber surveyed the owner hopefully and flagged them down. The woman pushing the wagon wore a ribbed dress with bells sewn into the fabric. Her cast-iron boots clanked heavily against the concrete floor and she brushed her shoulder pads and said, as if deprived of her own sight, "Is that the Overseer?"

"I am preoccupied with myself," answered Fibber. "As such, I doubt that you will be leaving me alone."

"I see a Tarasoff decision coming," said Malark as he rubbed his hands together. "You'll have to warn people about this patient..."

"My name is Julia Novikoff," said the woman. "My trade is that of the pistachio. Would you care for a sample?" She packed her hands with pistachios, threw them at Malark and Fibber and watched them bounce off of their bodies like droplets of wooden rain. Fibber caught one between his teeth, however, and said, "I'm starting to like this Overseer thing."

"You must have low standards to be swayed by a bucket of dried nuts," decided Malark.

"In the past, gods have been swayed by less." He threw another pistachio into his mouth. "To live for salted nuts is as good or bad as living for anything else. What about goulashes? What about tender aubergine cooked with salt and pepper and mozzarella? You ought to take food more seriously."

"Women are more likely to be supertasters. You love a good inconvenience," replied Malark as he discerned an urchin dragging an axe their way.

"Are you a writer?" asked Novikoff.

"I was," said Fibber as he worriedly gobbled pistachios, "these are great." It was then that Novikoff spat into her hand and rubbed Fibber's forehead.

Malark watched in disgust. "I can't sanction the erotic. But if you are willing to let these goats and monkeys clean you then be my guest—preferably over there."

"She is cleaning my forehead. What's wrong with that?" He gave her an innocent smile as he pressed her hand into his. "Thank you, madam."

"You are like that chap in *The Gypsy Baron*." Novikoff admired the Overseer and imagined him covered in gravy. "What I mean is that you are the chief gypsy and then you become the real baron. No baron can have mud on his face!" Turning her untapped anger onto her daughter she called after her. "Get over here! You little scamp!" Her daughter squirmed as she dragged her over. She was skinny and rough-looking and wearing a dress two sizes too big for her. The rings under her eyes punctuated the hollow cheeks and bordered her snub nose. Novikoff showed off her daughter to an increasingly disturbed Fibber. "Here is my one-time offer: marry my daughter. I know what you are thinking: she is as flat as a lake. But give her time and she will bud like any rose. In time she will be celestial. She will ripen and you will not be disappointed with the fruit." Her eyes narrowed. "For the love of the baron, your coat is dirty as well."

He pulled away from her. "How could you clean anything?"

Wiping his forehead of good intention he scowled and watched the axe-wielding urchin as he chopped logs.

"Getting a fire going!" hollered the urchin. His skin was the colour of custard and he wore an aviator's hat that covered his ears, eyebrows, and cheeks. "We are going to have some of that oink-oink!"

"Cut that wood, you geriatric youth!" commanded Malark as another log bit the dust. "As for you, Novikoff, why don't you comfort your daughter?"

"This one hates my cleaning and this one hates my comfort," complained Novikoff as two accusatory digits fled between chains. "What do you know about motherhood? You think I comfort because I can't clean? I clean because I can't comfort!"

"I used to be one," replied Malark. Then Fibber yanked him towards the staircase. "I've got to run!"

They ran toward the staircase under which a coterie of children had lodged themselves. Their leader was a small girl with one blind eye and missing teeth. She wore a ribbon in her hair and a worn yellow dress. "Are you two banging each other?" she asked Malark and Fibber as they ascended the staircase.

"I don't have to kill you because your spirits are all decrepit," Malark told the children. "Your fates are written on the stars and they are well and truly bleak."

But the children were unmoved by his words and threw pistachio shells. Pushing Malark up the staircase Fibber prevented Malark from doing anything regrettable.

As the cacophony of petulant children died away the stench of vaseline and hooch throttled Malark's nostrils. "The damp is much worse up here," muttered Malark. "I could plug these holes with Rachmaninov's hands."

Fibber oozed wisdom like a festering sore when he was bored. "I need a good hard woman...maybe a man...beggars can't be choosers."

Spotting a cockroach on the floor Malark got on his knees, poked his index finger into the boot-slick, and drew a circle around the insect. "These things don't care about meta-ethics. Why do we need moral terms like *good* and *right*—what is there to gain from them? I bet this cockroach doesn't give a damn about moral knowledge."

After only one morning of civil service duties Fibber and Malark had fallen back on cockroaches for company. "It's funny what this job does to you," commented Fibber.

Malark produced a sketchbook from his back pocket and started drawing the cockroach. "No clothes...no worrisome nudity...how quaint."

A woman of medium build appeared at the end of the corridor.

Fibber caught sight of her. "Beware! He'll paint you nude!"

"There's magic in the web of it," said the woman, after which she vanished. In his heart of hearts, Fibber believed that she had returned inside of a brothel.

Malark gave the cockroach a thumbs-up and the cockroach returned the gesture using its feelers and scuttled into a hole in the wall. "Are we going to have a rigid designator?" asked Malark.

Staring ponderously down the corridor, Fibber touched the soggy wall: "I have been told that there are women in the forests of Poland who run like foxes. They run circles around men and seduce them using their speed and charms—when they're not busy eating them…"

How many fairy tales were chauvinistic? Why was it that Fibber and Malark drew strength from them?

The Strongman and the Astrologer carried the combined luggage of the Metaphysical Circus. The other members walked on ahead along the staircase. A rumbling garnered their attention and then confusion when they could tell the sound emanated from the walls. The wall gave way and there came an avalanche of typewriters when they least expected it. The Maestro screamed and then the Bearded Lady swatted the Chicken Boy as it climbed onto his back. "Not my back!" screamed the Bearded Lady as his dress was torn to shreds. "You'll ruin everything!"

The avalanche subsided but everybody was buried. The talented limbs of the Metaphysical Circus stuck out like unlucky swans swimming in wet concrete. There was a cavalcade of clucking as the Maestro got the Chicken Boy under control. "Don't touch him! Leave my darling alone!" scolded the Maestro.

The Astrologer emerged from under a mound of typewriters. "Why do you worry about him? He doesn't need your stinking hands in his wallet. Like all pests, he is a survivor."

The Bearded Lady emerged subsequently and then ran his finger through the algae on the wall. He flicked a globule which tacked itself neatly to the Astrologer's eyebrow. "You're just jealous because the Chicken Boy is headlining."

"There's not going to be a show tonight you idiot. You think that because we're the only performers in here that we get carte blanche?" In frustration, the Astrologer kicked a typewriter. "Do you remember the meeting with the minister?"

"He's fine!" exclaimed the Maestro, relieved by the state of the Chicken Boy. "Thank God," he added as he prodigiously ignored the more developed human beings in his company.

Dusting a few typewriters off of his shoulders the Strongman squatted and fished a pouch of herb out of his pocket. "I'm fine too," said the Strongman as he pounded the herb into his pipe using his finger, lit the pipe, and sucked on it for a moment. "Thanks for asking."

"Who put these typewriters behind the wall?" Picking one up, the Maestro scrutinized it. Then he coughed and looked at the Strongman. "Put that pipe out, you chimpanzee."

"Steady," purred the Strongman as he puffed smoke. "The choice between dogmatism and idealism can't be made on theoretical grounds. What class of person do you think you are?"

"A man who has a thing for chickens," said the Astrologer. Minister Jozlov watched these goings-on from the bottom of the staircase. "Are you still here?" Then her eyes widened at the sight of the typewriters. "Did you damage them?" The Maestro guffawed and threw up his hands. "Did you *damage* them? Look at the state of my performers! I refuse to do anything if we have to do battle with wall-dwelling writing machines." He noticed a hint of liquorice in the Strongman's pipe-weed and winced.

"You are going to do what the Overseer tells you to do," reminded Jozlov.

"Then bring him here!" shouted the Astrologer. "Where the hell is he?"

"They don't give her that crystal ball for nothing," laughed the Strongman. "The Overseer seems to be as existent as God." Then he was distracted by the very thing that had urged him to smoke in the first place. "I'll be damned—what's with all these typewriters?"

"I haven't the faintest," peppered Jozlov. "But they will be government property if they are in here."

"I don't see custom stamps," stated the Maestro as he pretended to look. "I would bet my life that they are made in China and smuggled in during the night. For what reason?"

The Astrologer shook her head and opened her suitcase where she extracted a zither-like instrument. "I'm going to do a Bolingbroke," she said. "I am going to see if there is a balance to be struck between artistic expression and philosophical penetration." Plucking the strings, she began to hum a sad song.

The Maestro pleaded with her to stop. "There'll be none of that crap in my circus. Our methods are locally sourced."

Jozlov tossed a crushed sweet wrapper to the ground. "There is a Japanese insect spirit who parties around cucumbers. The legend is that a physician got himself stuck in a cucumber vine where he got killed by some villain."

The Strongman giggled and dropped his pipe onto the ground. "Cucumbers!" He slapped his forehead and laughed. "Big cucumbers!"

"If we could gamble we wouldn't have to recycle costumes," added the Bearded Lady.

"And you wonder why I talk about firing you," said the Maestro. "Try to be more like the Chicken Boy."

"He's only got one costume, you prestigious jerk."

Jozlov clapped her hands at the end of the staircase and pointed to the typewriters. "Make sure that you pile them neatly. I'll see to it that they're moved."

"Why didn't you move them from our bodies?" asked the Maestro. Before he had finished complaining Minister Jozlov had simultaneously disappeared behind shadows and the burnished light offered by high-hanging hydrogen lamps. "Damn you!" exclaimed the Maestro.

The Astrologer continued playing as the Strongman gasped with laughter. "What a crestfallen kettle of fish we are," he wheezed.

"BOGACK!" announced the Chicken Boy. The noise caught everyone off-guard and the Astrologer stopped playing and there were tears in her eyes.

The brothel on the second floor was a hub of activity. There was a table topped with boiled meats and vegetables which people visited at their leisure before returning to fornication behind suspended Turkish carpets. The smells were as intense as they were illegal, and hydrogen lamps emptied their light across the coughing, sweating, and shifting chamber.

There was a man called Levitsky who beat a tambourine. He wore a leather tunic and nylon trousers which swished as he moved to his beat. His eyes were too close together and he had a crown of white hair and a white goatee. "It's Thursday!" he cheered as he danced around the room. "I used to know Mary Magdalene!" Then he paused briefly to stoke the fire on the other side of the room. After this, he banged his tambourine again, ignoring the pain in his knees, and sang,

Plum Lukuuuuuum!
Sweet death, what is your tune?
Will it make me sweet, make me sick?
Cut my hair, give a stick
To beat—to beeeeeat—the politicians!

Plum Lukuuuuuum!
Belgian Queen, where's my tomb?
Will I sleep alone, with a girl?
Under filth, my hair in curls
For strangling—strangliiiiiing—politicians!

Aroused and semi-naked, Malark struggled against the waves of his own physical performance. "Levitsky is walking on thin ice," panted Malark over an unlucky prostitute who had received the greatest instruction from her boss on how to conceal her boredom and was doing so admirably as the arrogant deputy overseer wriggled hither and thither on top of her. The prostitute's name was Oksana and she had pale skin, a wide mouth, thick caterpillar-like eyebrows, and short hair. "We only let him out once a week," explained the bored prostitute.

"Don't tell me." His pathetic attempts at locomotion buffeted his words. "To sing?"

"No, to bathe us—"

Malark sprang up in horror and skidded over the floor as the Turkish carpets collapsed and revealed Oksana's disappointed face. "How awful! Yuck!" shrieked Malark.

Oksana lied about enjoying her time with Malark and slipped into a loose-fitting tunic. "There's nothing I like better than a nice fat doughy pecker. You give me a plaster cast and I can get to work."

Malark had the melancholy and the stupor of the Dark Ages and he imagined that if he started dancing the Dark Ages would re-appear altogether. Instead he grabbed a potato and threw it at the old man, Levitsky, who took the poisonous nightshade projectile like a champ.

"Lucky shot," said Levitsky, after which he stuck out his tongue.

"You're surreal. I cannot take you seriously," replied Malark. But no one was listening because they were looking at Malark's genitals which were like chairs on public transport.

Meanwhile, an architect was wandering around the brothel. He wore an army helmet and a silk robe which was secured by a snakeskin belt. "If you squeeze a potato it will give you luck," he said as he bumbled past Oksana, squeezing maggots out of a piece of beef that he had acquired from the reeking table.

"You're too realistic for me to fall in love with you," said Oksana to Malark. "If you have any decency you will not ask me if I have a boyfriend."

"Don't worry, Oksana!" announced a centenarian prostitute farming lichen under a table. Her hair was bright white and sat on her oddly shaped head like a dollop of ice cream. She was also wearing a green catsuit that was three sizes too large for her. "I'm going to make us some lichen tea. It should be fine. I gave some to Levitsky and he is still alive!"

Passing the partition Levitsky banged his tambourine and laughed. "Sita won that archery contest," he said as he stumbled to the other side of the room.

On the other side of the brothel, Fibber had just finished making love to a prostitute called Yulia who had short dark hair, large ears, and thin eyebrows. She was short and she had large hands and large feet. Hidden by their Turkish carpet, they watched as a nosy prostitute passed by the cracks in the curtain and stared at them. "You stare at her and she stares back," said the mossy prostitute on the other side. "That is when the sex comes: not from the front but from the side."

Fibber laughed as Yulia examined his hairy feminine pectorals. "That old chap of yours, Levitsky, must have studied anthropology."

"It's habit-strength. The bond between stimulus and response." The hairy feminine pectorals pleased her and she contained a burp. "Your deputy hasn't learned a damn thing. He doesn't seem the type."

He patted the sweat forming under one pectoral. "In keeping with his style."

Watching him, Yulia formed questions. "You are the new Overseer?"

Retrieving his green coat, he covered both himself and Yulia. "It's the same colour as those algae on the ceiling— And no, I never dream of discounts."

"In places like this you will find only anathema," replied Yulia. "Have you any idea what you are overseeing?"

"You, Malark, Oksana, Minister Jozlov. She could be in here for all I care." He viewed the twinkling algae between his finger pads. "I think that they ought to have more writers in the civil service. We lock into systems that have had the logic squeezed out of them. I don't bother myself with rationality and neither, it appears, do you. The best example is Plum Lukum...if we defeated her on the coast, this place wouldn't exist."

"My feeling is that the Tectum was built before Plum Lukum. I suppose most writers keep their heads under rocks," insisted Yulia.

"We're looking for moss."

"Moss grows on rocks—not under them."

"Not always."

On the other side, Levitsky had decided to compose a motet for tambourines. He asked people for suggestions and someone said he should hang himself.

"In the Tectum we have reasons for being here," said Yulia. "But none of them have anything to do with Plum Lukum. We don't understand the threat that we are facing. A statement like that is more infrequent than the sort of question which prompts it." Distracted by her cynicism she parted the hanging Turkish carpet.

Yulia could see the architect seated with a ladle propped under his chin.

"Anybody got any pepper?" he asked the woman next to him. She was wearing a shoe on her head and she tied the laces under her jaw and stared him squarely in the eye. "I met Buzz Aldrin once when I snorted some," came her reply.

Just then a comment from Fibber reclaimed the intimacy between Yulia and himself. "Don't bend your spine," warned Fibber. "You'll get Hurler's Syndrome faster than I can read *Othello*, though I would rather find some scissors."

There came the sound of a kerfuffle on the other side of the brothel. Malark had abandoned all hope of maintaining an erection and was buckling his trousers. "I have had enough…forget it."

Oksana opened the gap in the Turkish carpet and addressed her colleagues as they ate raw onions and picked at their noses affably. "The purse of the deputy overseer is shallower than he would first accept," laughed Oksana.

"What is the purpose of money if not for buying things?" Malark asked, addressing the partition behind which were Fibber and Yulia. "It was public money and made for spending."

The exhausted Fibber made to stand. "Come back tonight," said Yulia with an outstretched hand. "Come back."

He touched her cheek. Then he poked his head out of the partition and said, "Dress no further, Malark, I am on my way!"

Gradually the Overseer gathered his clothes and finally joined his deputy.

"You are late," commented Malark as he discerned a carrot between Fibber's thighs.

"Oh no!" yelled Fibber. "I came too late!" Pretending as though the carrot were uncontrollable, Fibber kicked his feet. "It won't stop! Somebody! Help me!"

The groups who were discussing the fair price for de-weevilled bread turned and laughed at the crazy sight of Fibber holding a carrot between his legs.

Incensed at being upstaged Levitsky beat his tambourine harder. "A life in showbusiness…when showtime comes you shall have to do better than that…"

Malark observed Fibber's performance and said, "You're a child."

"I'm finished," said Fibber, after which he traded the carrot for trousers. Then he donned his upper half and approached the woman whom his deputy had failed to reimburse.

"That minister of yours believes the economy will collapse," said Oksana.

"You are not going to lure me back with talk of economics," shouted Malark from the distance, "they tried the same with Thomas Jefferson when America was a sick infant."

("Brief psychotherapy," decided Yulia.)

"The economy can sink to the bottom of the Parliamentary Sea," replied Fibber. "I am trying to hold this place together using bits of gum and good luck."

Yulia stood over a basin filled with warm water and washed her groin. "How is that going?"

Watching her with an erotic interest that was not wholly disrespectful Fibber continued his assessment. "This place needs prolonged psychotherapy. Maybe electro-shock. We might even put on a play. We have to distract those rowdy residents. Not you fine ladies, of course."

The centenarian in the green catsuit sidled up next to Fibber where she cupped his groin and whistled merrily into the piecemeal bureaucratic ear, "Playtime...?"

"It looks as though you already have your hands full," replied Fibber as he accelerated in the opposite direction, "but it's impossible to have a surplus of sex because it's natural."

"Thank you," said Yulia who contemplated cooking Fibber for some reason. "You are a *natural* man. You are always welcome here."

The woman wearing the shoe on her head was upset. She was being patted on the back by the architect who spent half the time looking over his shoulder. "I've lost my sense of smell," sniffed the woman as she dropped a bloody peppershaker to the filthy ground.

"Malark has all the human qualities of a stapler," buzzed Oksana.

Then the deputy overseer said a very nasty thing back which made Fibber wince.

"For God's sake, Malark," said Fibber as he tempered the crowd with his hands.

Oksana turned round and parted her bum cheeks wide. "Er hat keine Bälle!"

Malark thought long and hard about what to do. He decided that a joke might remedy the situation which he had created. "What is the difference between a Turk and a Bavarian? The Turk can speak better German."

Oksana turned around and said, "I am from Dusseldorf, you limp noodle!"

"Naturally," said Malark as a piece of boiled beef splotched at his base of his wellington boot. "An Englishman and a German are building houses and they place a bet on who is going to finish first. Three weeks pass and the Englishman says, Just five more days until I'm finished! To which the German says, Just five more forms to fill out before I can start!" Laughing at his joke, he concluded, "It is no surprise that your clothes came off so slowly. You were doing forms in the back."

In the meantime, Levitsky had been remembering the Protestant songs of old. He picked one out from his memory, raised his arms, and said,

Auf Christen, singt festliche Lieder
Und jauchzet mit fröhlichem Klang!
Es halle auf Erden laut wider
Hell tönender Jubelgesang!

The architect blew out a candle. He tapped the helmet protecting his head and nodded with pleasure at the ceiling. "Just checking," he said as he replaced the pepper shaker.

Yulia had finished using the basin to clean herself and Malark picked it up and overturned the basin onto Levitsky's head. "We can have some quiet now," said Malark.

The men laughed but the women said nothing. Unmoved by male humour they voiced their chagrin through their silence.

Fibber clipped the back of Malark's head—and the deputy overseer stumbled forward, gathering his startled senses, and subsequently recovered his footing with fury in his eyes.

Why were parents who did the same to their children surprised when they grew up being surprised by nothing?

"Two muffins are baking together in an oven," began Fibber. "One of them says to the other, Is it hot in here or is it just me? The other muffin says, My God! A talking muffin!"

"What about the other muffins?" asked Malark.

Raising an eyebrow Fibber wiggled his fingers, "Go away."

Oksana was bored and decided to have a bath. There was, after all, such a thing as having too much baked potato in one's hair.

Meanwhile the architect approached Levitsky who had removed the basin and was drying his head with another man's sock.

"Look at this noggin," said the architect as he removed his helmet and tapped three times on his bald and scabby scalp. "Come and have a go at it—you bastard..."

Entering the fourth floor the Metaphysical Circus found a giant space with a domed ceiling. Before his employees could rest the Maestro ordered them to inflate the incredible circus tent. To do this the mammoth tent was unpacked and then unrolled after which a circuit of pumps were connected around the perimeter of the tent. To inflate the tent the Strongman, the Bearded Lady, and the Astrologer ran along the circuit as the tent slowly began to rise like a giant cake.

Ignoring them, the Maestro and the Chicken Boy lounged before the covered wagon. The Maestro was wearing a sunhat and reading *Othello*. The Chicken Boy was wearing sunglasses and stared dimly through crooked lenses.

On the fifteenth circuit, the Astrologer's feet started to blister. "I'm sick of this," she gasped through tired teeth. "Why do we always do this?"

"Be quiet," ordered the Maestro in the distance. "I must concentrate."

Running still, the Strongman showed solidarity by smiling. "This soufflé takes ages to inflate. It's not bad when you've got long legs like mine." He looked behind at the Bearded Lady who was bouncing towards him. "How is she doing?"

"She?" objected the Bearded Lady. "Where have you been?"

"I'll get used to it," insisted the puffing Strongman. "Sorry."

"It comes across as rude."

"The world comes across as rude," gasped the Astrologer ahead of him.

"The world is rude. But hear me out," said the Strongman. "In the past you filled the role of the Bearded Lady. You were very good at it. But now that you've changed gender—" He picked his words carefully. "The problem is that there's nothing remarkable about a bearded man. We'd be the same if I grew a beard."

"What's your point, big boy?" The Bearded Lady caught up.

"A bearded lady has novelty." Nervously the Strongman raised his hands. "But a bearded man is just normal."

"Neptune saves the King of Crete. But in return, the King has to kill the first person he meets. He bumps into someone and kills them. But that person turns out to be his son."

Rolling her eyes, the Astrologer used her prodigious memory. "He is recalling Mozart's opera which had a Frenchman's libretto."

"How does he not recognize his son?" asked the Strongman.

The tent swelled with air.

"Lady Harriet pretends to be a servant called Martha and hires herself out at the Richmond Fair," responded the Bearded Lady.

"Fine! Ignore me! I await the day when you realize that you have as much novelty as a four-legged cat," choked the Strongman. "In the meantime, put cotton in your ears."

The tent croaked to life and soon it was on the verge of exploding.

"BOGACK." The sunglasses fell from the Chicken Boy's face and the Maestro tore off his sunhat like a frog usurping an unwanted lily-pad. Hopping to his feet, the Maestro stomped his boots on the concrete ground. "How dare you frighten my prized possession? The tent will explode! Get off those pumps!"

Sagging alongside his two exhausted colleagues the Strongman collapsed on the floor where he breathed heavily and wished he were outside. They had weathered storms and riots and ungrateful audiences. "How can the Maestro be worse?" whispered the Strongman.

Kicking a log from the fire, the Maestro shook his fist. "Do you see what you have done to my Chicken Boy? I shall have to relax him now…b-but never mind that." He checked for eavesdroppers and then nodded to himself. "You have to understand that without him we are finished. We might as well visit the brothel and offer up our services. My body is sacred!"

Spotting a book in the Maestro's hands, the Strongman saw a black man strangling a white woman on the cover. "Have I been in the employ of a racist?"

"What in the name of Ishmael are you discussing?" frothed the Maestro.

"Are we doing naughty shows?"

"No..." begged the Astrologer.

"I'm reading Othello, you dunce. It's a real dollop of tripe," declared the Maestro.

"Oh...Shakespeare..." He relaxed. "I just thought... Nicholas Sparks..." He passed out.

In the wasteland, Marielle Agapov walked for miles. The rain whipped her body as she stepped through moss and shrubs. Having decided it would be suicide to return from whence she came she aimed for the Black Forest and could see the dark tips massing on the horizon. She could feel the mud drying on her legs as she watched the sky beginning to freeze over.

"He deserved to die." She plodded through the grass. "But look where it got me. An improvement. Cook all day, every day, not even the food I liked. He had to like the food that went on the table. It's all the more reason for him to cook." She traced over what had brought her to murder her husband. He had accused her of trying to kill him when he noticed the pork was undercooked. "It was *perfect*...perfectly cooked." She lost her footing and fell into a sandy clearing which was depressed and barren.

Using her sleeve to clean her face, she spotted a thatched door on the edge. "Impossible." Sprinting across the clearing she got to the other side where she shook the door. "Help me! It will be night soon and I'm freezing. I don't want to die in this hellhole. I haven't a single weapon on me!"

A reedy voice on the other side replied, "Go away..."

"But you must help me." Agapov protested. "There is a storm brewing. There is nothing I can do to stop it."

"What do you want?"

"Forgiveness!"

The door opened to reveal an old woman whose mouth contained three teeth and whose dim eyes oversaw the world. Her hair was long and shaggy and seemed to be every possible colour of hair. Her skin flaked and wept in alternating patches and she was wearing a filthy undershirt and a shabby leather overcoat creased with age. There were moss-coloured boots on her disfigured feet and overall, she cut a hunchbacked figure whose body had been twisted by resentment. "Because you found an obliging soul you will be forgiven for the dastardly deed you committed…though obligation and hypocrisy are vacant in my veins."

"Please, it's cold."

"Tourists are disallowed," vented the old woman.

"Please." Kneeling in the mud Agapov tugged at the woman's dress. "They refused to let me inside of the Tectum."

"How does one like you fail to be admitted to a sanatorium?" Her eyes betrayed knowledge and she quickly changed tack. "You must leave this place."

"Where am I supposed to go?"

"You are content to leave but have no direction? You are like static liquid. An excellent case study for hydrostatics. Meanwhile, hydrodynamics, the study of moving liquid, is much simpler than you are. You are *mercurial*."

Why were women so cruel to one another? thought Agapov.

"I killed my husband!"

Above them, frothy rain plummeted from the sky and drenched their skin. "Did you know," replied the old woman, "that there are children who believe that they were born through their mother's anus? It is called Cloaca Theory. Who are these children? Who are their parents? That is something I should like to know."

With nothing to verify this woman's madness, Agapov returned the conversation to herself. "You don't believe me? About my husband?"

"What if I do, child?"

"Let me in—" She pushed past the old woman.

She found herself in a dark cramped space dotted by candlelight and a single vent that sang melancholy songs because it opened onto the wasteland. There was a make-shift stove in the corner in which she could see red embers flashing in the dark. Maps crackled on the walls and a lonely wooden table in the centre of the room creaked from the gradual change in temperature afforded by the open door. In the corner of the cave was a collection of hay and blankets which served as a mattress and adjacent, almost as a warning, was a bucket and spade scented with lavender picked outside.

"Get out," growled the old woman who moved rapidly toward her. "You have no right. You will get us both killed."

"Why do I know your face?" She broke away from the old woman. She imagined she was a dissident who had been banished to the wasteland.

"Do you see better in the dark?" The old woman reached out as if to grab something.

"You have a name, don't you?"

"My name...is Plum Lukum." Shutting the door she sulked in semi-darkness, folding her bony arms and protecting the heat her soul had been denied.

In the basement, the furnace room glowed like a recently erupted volcano. Dozens of men and women wearing boiler suits carried hydrogen cubes from heap to furnace and then burned whatever came down the garbage chutes.

The foreman was called Kosha. He was a small man who wore a bright red boiler suit stained with ash. He wore heat-resistant goggles to protect his eyes and clomped around the furnace room in his oversized Wellington boots. Noting the dwindling number of hydrogen cubes, Kosha unzipped his boiler suit, opened a toolbox, and removed a bowl of pistachios. He sat on the toolbox and tossed the salted nuts into his mouth.

A furnace worker with orange goggles and charred hair stepped over. "Any good?"

"Taste like barbiturates," said Kosha as he frowned in his underwear and ignored the beads of sweat dripping from his face onto the concrete ground.

The worker laughed, picked up a mattress and lobbed it into the furnace. "You never get back to sleep when you wake up on sleeping pills," she said as she tapped her goggles.

At that moment, Fibber and Malark entered the furnace room.

"Self-contained," noted Fibber as they strode towards the centre of the blistering room. "The vegetables will keep in any case. Not too sure about the people."

A worker wearing knee-length aluminium boots and a bra coughed suggestively. "The bosses are here! They want dancing!" He banged two spoons together and kicked up his heels dramatically.

"Get back to work!" Malark threw a bin bag at a furnace worker who lobbed it into the furnace.

Workers gathered around Kosha as he became the centre of attention. Muttering rude things about their visitors, the furnace workers watched Malark as he approached them.

"If you gave these monkeys sketch pads they wouldn't produce an exhibition. Nor would they cope with the quagmire of galleries taking fifty percent commission," said Malark as he itched at his plastic chain mail and confronted the foreman. "Are you the foreman?"

"These are my nuts." Kosha nibbled a pistachio. "I have twenty minutes every hour for snack time according to the union rulebook. My workers have done nothing wrong. They have no quarrel with you, deputy overseer…if that is your official title?"

Was this why Malark had refused to join the union of artists?

Malark took the bag of pistachios and threw them into the furnace. "A brief demonstration of combustion. Your foreman thinks he invented it," said the deputy overseer.

Having learned to give his deputy the dirty work, Fibber kicked through the rubbish. Why had the upstairs people thrown out all these books? A staggering number of books!

Biting his thumbnail, Fibber picked up *Giovanni's Room*. "In the same way that you think you invented painting," asked Fibber. "Who would get rid of *Giovanni's Room?*" (A worker was whistling to herself and pretended to be innocent when in reality she was slipping three James Baldwin novels into her rucksack, after which she zipped up the fly.)

"A man who is not gay," laughed Malark.

"You are as complex as apple pie," replied Fibber as he pounded towards him. "*Giovanni's Room* is not about gay people. It's about everyone and the ability to love them."

He ruffled his overcooked afro and stood before the foreman as he licked his dry lips. "Greetings, foreman. I wish to inform you that this book is going into my pocket." He pocketed *Giovanni's Room*. "Is there anything else I should know?"

"Zurück zur Arbeit, Leute," ordered Kosha.

The workers returned to their clambering and the chamber glowed with combustion.

Kosha quietly prevented himself from being sick. "If the constants of theoretical physics were a little different the universe wouldn't be here," he said. "It wouldn't exist and neither would we. The fine-tuning of these constants is so unlikely that it makes no sense to attribute them to mere chance. There's more sense in attributing their synchronicity to intelligent design—or God."

Malark clomped over. "Look at his red eyes. He does nothing but read. He ought to be throwing crap in that furnace. But what does he do? He sits around telling stories instead."

"I have a right to read. How will I survive if I don't educate myself?"

"Eat when you're hungry. Get enough sleep. Have sex. Don't kill anyone who isn't worth it," mandated Malark.

"Where did you read about God?" The tone of Fibber's voice was fragile.

"When people came in this morning, the first thing they did was throw out all of their books. You can tell that these books came from the poor folk because they have much better taste. They came down the chutes. We burn them with the hydrogen cubes because the cubes are running out. I pocket a novel or a dictionary only occasionally. You can call it my hobby." Standing slowly the foreman cupped his mouth and whispered secretively. "I have an idea why everyone is here, Overseer."

"Plum Lukum is why everyone is here," stated Fibber.

"That's the official reason," prattled Malark.

"You two," hissed Fibber as he glared between Malark and Kosha. "I want to get out of here with all of my limbs still attached to my body. Do you two understand? Comrade foreman and deputy overseer?"

Above them, a worker laughed and rubbed Vaseline on his dark skin. "If you can't stand the heat, stay out of the furnace."

"How did he get up there?" asked Fibber vacantly.

Kosha poked the Overseer's chest. "Your head is only within this head," he said. "There are several thousand heads upstairs. Or don't their heads matter?"

"What's this hypothesis knocking about in *your* head?" Fibber sighed and watching the furnace, wondered when everyone he knew would either be dead or dying.

Kosha stepped into his boiler suit and zipped the bright red material shut. He beckoned Malark and Fibber to stroll with him by the dwindling stacks of hydrogen cubes and rubbish. "Your deputy jogged my memory when he called us monkeys," he said as he listened to their combined conspiratorial footsteps. "Imagine a vast assembly of monkeys. They each have a typewriter and press the keys at random. We can assume it's unlikely that one of them will produce a line from Shakespeare because we would have to wait a phenomenally long time for that to happen. These monkeys would have to type for centuries. But the point being, Overseer—"

"Yes?"

"—is that we don't think monkeys wrote *Othello*. Instead, we think Shakespeare sat down with ink and quill and wrote every line. In other words, he designed it himself. But the physical universe is way more unlikely than monkeys producing *Othello* after a million years of typing."

"Uh-huh."

"It's just as unreasonable to think that *Othello* happened randomly as it is to think the universe happened randomly. It's especially unreasonable with *Othello* because it takes millions of years for order to arise from chaos. That's God's work cut out, you see?"

"I have to say," said Malark as he pinched his nose, "there's never been a better argument for burning the works of Shakespeare."

Fibber sucked his teeth and said, "You turn everything into a joke. You would have died years ago without jokes. So? What is the idea within the idea, Kosha?"

Shadow and light clashed across Kosha's face. "Undesirables have been collected to prove the existence of God by making them hammer away on typewriters," he summed up as he shrugged the positivity out of his body. "I know it's unlikely now. But will it be just as unlikely in a thousand years?"

"I signed a bloody contract," said Fibber as he contemplated how long he would be here. "Are there typewriters?"

"I've heard rumours. We haven't had any come down the chute. But all that means is that people aren't throwing them out. If they end up down here, I'm going to melt them down. With God as my witness."

Some junk rattled down the rubbish slope towards them. A heavy-set worker with a yellow boiler suit and ferocious eyebrows seemed to speak to the ceiling. "Glory to the workers!"

Malark put his arms around Fibber and Kosha and guided the men back to the toolbox. "Three comrades are chatting in the furnace room. One of them is being provocative and the other two are telling jokes. One joker says, You shouldn't be so provocative. The Bluebloods have everything wired for sound. The provocative guy shrugs and says, Come on, that's bullshit. There's nothing to worry about. The other joker says, It's not! Watch! He snaps his fingers and says, minister, three cups of coffee! Without warning the doors open and people arrive with coffee. The three comrades are shocked and go to sleep. The next morning the provocateur is missing. Only the jokers are left. One of them finds Minister Jozlov and asks what happened to his friend. She says,

The Bluebloods took him last night. The joker asks why he and his friend were spared. The minister says, We really liked your coffee prank!"

"Cynic," said Fibber as he detached himself from Malark and made to leave.

"Remember which side your bread is buttered," said Malark as he slapped Kosha's bum. He then joined Fibber at the entrance and waved awkwardly at the furnace workers.

"Remind me to get you a typewriter," whispered Fibber as they straddled the staircase and disappeared.

Kosha lowered his goggles and then returned to work. "Listen up, folks! I want the Christie and the Simenon in the furnace. They may be tiddlers but they number greatly. But don't touch *The Koran*. I want all those holy books intact; do you hear me?"

The wasteland was dark and the stars above were anathema. The clearing in which Plum Lukum had fashioned her hovel glowed and a weak gleam cut through the thatched door.

Agapov watched Lukum ladle grass soup into mugs. The sight was painful because she was starving. She considered how tough Lukum might be after roasting her with wild garlic and grass oil for thirty minutes.

"The soup has no body. It is the only recipe that I have," said Lukum as she passed the mug. "It is hard to invent with grass. Sometimes the occasional rabbit. I have tried catching them but they are faster than you think."

"Thank you." Agapov eyed the soup and forgot how long she had been there.

"You are not welcome. But you need food," sighed Lukum.

"It's your home," said Agapov diplomatically.

"How could anyone lay claim to this nest? This is not my home. This is my punishment." Looking through the vent she spotted the stars.

"You're not Belgian?"

"My great-grandparents were Belgian. If I'm Belgian, then most of England is foreign to itself. I have no intention of conquering this miserable place. I am from the city," said Lukum as she managed a chuckle. "Watching the stars... each circle has a centre of symmetry and the symmetry guides me home. I have to accept how far I have come. Once upon a time, I was the Minister for Transport. I eke out a life in the wastelands now because I have been punished."

Agapov realized a dissident was feeding her grass soup. "What must you have done to get banished to this place?" Then she eyed the soup for any doughy film left by poison.

Lukum startled. Her eyes had lost the ability to measure.

"I have waited so long to discuss crime and punishment," said Lukum. "I disapproved when they converted some two hundred public buses to military vehicles without my knowledge or consent. That is why I am here. I wished to prevent murder. But you carried one out. We both have dismal views of people. They are stupid enough to need protecting. But you believe that they are stupid enough to kill. We created the study of metaphysics to investigate reality, existence, substance, and causality. What use is metaphysics when a man has been murdered? If we cannot inform our decisions using sensory experience then what *can* we use? I know it is wrong to feel pathos for you. Aristotle confined the feeling to art."

Agapov slurped her soup. "We've both sinned."

"I assign neither sins nor blessings. But we *have* sinned." She paused. "Why…did you kill your husband?"

"He beat me and my children."

"You did what you had to do." Outside an object or creature creaked in the wind. "A solution presented itself. Or did you kneel before the solution?" She smiled. "I shall stop analysing you. I have always wondered what constitutes the opposite of reification. Perhaps reducing a woman to a single memory constitutes that process." Her guilt was well-developed.

"What is the Tectum?" asked Agapov.

"According to Aboriginal folklore, the Wandjina created the very first human beings. They were disgusted with their creations and vomited and the vomit became a flood that washed away the first humans. Then the Wandjina started over. They created a second race that they designed to behave correctly…as they saw fit…the final solution was an experiment. Who knows how many times the Wandjina repeated this process…?"

Agapov gagged on her soup.

"It did not rain on the day they came for me," continued Lukum. "The Minister of Defence oversaw my eviction while he allowed his deputy to beat my husband. They tossed his body into the street when they had finished beating him and set it aflame. Then they burnt my books on his body. It was explained to me that I had committed crimes of terrorism. But it is impossible to be innocent when you have as many rules as we do. My first punishment would be the use of my name for this invisible threat. They lectured the public that I had left the country and raised an army. A human being created that lie as well as this—the second punishment...look around you..."

"How sad," said Agapov dully.

"I long for death. You will do this for me."

The wind howled and the fire died down.

A hard day's work had sent the Metaphysical Circus to bed early. In the covered wagon the Maestro, the Bearded Lady, and the Chicken Boy snored peacefully and occasionally kicked one another.

The circus tent smelled of asbestos and was no place to sleep. A lack of room in the covered wagon had forced the Strongman and the Astrologer to purchase a two-man tent.

After zipping the tent's entrance, they did the same to their sleeping bags. The tent was too small and their legs went numb and they regretted using their wages to purchase the smaller tent.

"We had enough money for a bigger tent months ago." Curling her toes the Astrologer felt the life draining out of them. "Where did it go?"

"Chicken feed. Are you warm?"

"I'm numb on one side...I'm warm."

"A man would be hard-pressed to fit two dwarves into this tent," smirked the Strongman. "I would be more comfortable sleeping next to the Chicken Boy."

"The Maestro wouldn't permit that."

"He doesn't have to worry about me sharpening my knives. He looks chewy. I like pork better anyway." He smiled and parlayed his disappointment into a better thought.

"Cheeky," said the Astrologer as she massaged her numb foot. "Once upon a time, the King of Boeotia entertained Hermes, Poseidon, and Zeus. He desperately wanted a child and asked them to give him one. The King had a bull's hide and the Gods pissed on it. He buried the hide and afterwards, a child came out of the earth whom the King named Orion."

"What a bedtime story." Puffing his chest, the Strongman blew his nose.

"Orion was a giant...like you."

"Orion's father wasn't a poor furrier. Mine left me in a box when I was but a babe. I always like to think it did me some good. But looking at this tent I can't help but think he was right."

No answer came. The Strongman saw that she had fallen asleep. He laid back and smiled. "Good night, Orion..."

The table was populated by food and drink when Fibber and Malark returned to the brothel. Greeting Fibber with a raucous hug, Yulia dragged him behind the Turkish carpet where they quickly made love. The rowdy crowd of regulars beyond the partition drank ale and chewed on boiled meats.

Smiling over her naked body Fibber believed that no police would interrupt him.

Levitsky dipped between guests and peeked around Yulia's partition. She had finished making love to Fibber when Levitsky banged his tambourine and sang,

> The girls are unclothed
> Such is the butter of creep-joints
> Greater is Fibber's globing
> Of his purchased betrothed
> Then his deputy's fight
> With a floppy stalactite
> Ill repute always anoints
> This chirping chamber—its wet hands
> We gather up these unborn babes
> Slaughtered from thy glands!

The crowd applauded spilling drink and food and soon forgot the whole affair. "He must have had an education! He must have a sense of responsibility!" said a woman with two spiked gloves and a hammock full of fresh fruit. Levitsky knew that they were too young to remember the glory days of the Security Bureau when he had patrolled the streets in a pressed uniform with polished leather boots and gloves. "Another song!" announced Levitsky as he parked his memories to one side of his duplicitous brain.

"We're going to need that damn bucket again," said Fibber as he laughed with Yulia. "You would need ten thousand buckets," said Yulia as they restored their lovemaking.

In the crowd, the architect banged an orange against his helmet and swore at himself. "Damn this walnut," he said as he examined the object. "Oh...wait a minute..."

Levitsky visited the sexual exploits of Oksana and her monetarily and sexually disadvantaged client. He peered around the partition and watched Malark having sex. He cleared his throat and sang,

> In limbo were his songs
> For, in them, stank descriptions
> Chickens roasted, lamb and cheese
> Figs erect and worth a kiss
> Then later foggy heads
> A morning's day hooked on dread
> Crow's feet like grave inscriptions

On the verge of orgasm, Malark struggled to finish.

> Hailed are songs in flairs forgotten
> Motions in despair neglected
> For, ghosts are begotten
> Then, loosely, forgotten

"Thank God that's over," said Oksana.

"His songs are terrible," replied Malark who misinterpreted her meaning. He was ignorant to the fact that he had just supplied the worst intercourse in the history of the world.

Oksana admired him with scientific curiosity.

Standing up Malark marched to the table where he knocked over plates and cups. "You should do a Strong Interest Inventory," Malark told Levitsky as he tore into a piece of meat. The meat squirted a phlegm of fat into someone's eye who screamed and ran in circles.

The architect observed the victim of Malark's meat, tapped his helmet, and sighed. "Ivan lost his eye to a lamb chop last week," said the architect as he poured cold wine onto the victim's face, practically gouged the man's eyes out, and then sat down thinking he was brave.

Malark grunted. What were these people good for? He would have found better company in the southern prospects.

"The angle between two sides of a polygon lying within a polygon," described Oksana. "A salient angle appears when the interior angle is less than one hundred and eighty degrees." She looked squarely at Malark who returned the sorry gaze. "I'm talking about your balls. Is there a doctor in the house?"

Malark threw a bone at her and she threw it straight back hitting Malark's neck. "Too bad that didn't kill me." He paused and listened to the other side of the room. "People are trying to eat, Fibber—keep the noise down."

"Leave him alone. He's having fun," supplied Oksana.

Meanwhile, Fibber and Yulia orgasmed simultaneously. "A rare feat," cheered Yulia.

"Any good?" asked Fibber shyly.

Yulia laughed when people dropped coins over the partition. Training her eyes on Fibber she stuck out her tongue. "You are not a classical man. You are not serene. You are neither neo-classical nor rational. I think you are one of those troubled romantics with no interest in harmony or constraint." She paused. "But where is your expression?"

"I had an inkling the sex fulfilled that."

"You will have unhealthy expression if you only express yourself through sex. Where there's emotionalism there will be nothing but frost. Where there's spontaneity there will be nothing but calculation. Where there's imagination there will be nothing but pedestrianism. The originality which you had within your poetry will dry out and become common-place. You will be a conformist!" she vented with frustration.

"You've been listening to Levitsky for too long," remarked Fibber. "You have become a romantic. I could never date a romantic."

"You are a reluctant romantic at heart. I would love to discard you like a used flip-flop but I can't. Not just yet," confirmed Yulia.

"I thought I was good in bed?"

"You were trying too hard," replied Yulia.

"She's right," said Malark as he peeked through the partition, "I was watching."

Fibber leapt up and knocked the partition over. He pushed Malark into the table where his gut connected with the grease-covered wood and Malark went down like a sack of potatoes.

Fibber half-carried, half-dragged Malark to a chair. Acquiring a watermelon from the fruit merchant's soggy hammock Fibber sliced the thing in half and screwed the abused fruit onto Malark's head.

Awaking slowly, Malark laughed as Fibber drank leisurely from a tankard of ale. Would they care if he killed Malark? Would they exact their revenge on him afterwards?

Malark watched Fibber sarcastically.

"What do *you* want?" asked Fibber.

The watermelon rocked on Malark's head. "You were carrying out some co-twin control experiment. You wanted to see if hereditary factors could be controlled between us. You don't understand? You beat the crap out of one twin and leave the other one alone. This is my question…can you feel the watermelon on your head?"

The architect watched with interest and squished a fly on his shoulder. "Jesus Christ isn't real but his brother is," he noted with scientific accuracy. "I banged him last century."

"A twin calls his brother from prison," continued Malark. "The twin says, So, you know how we finish each other's sentences…?"

"Shut up, Malark." Fibber squinted.

"He told his brother to shut up. What a tragedy. Come over here, Levitsky."

"*Our brain is within a brain. The living like the dead,*" recited Levitsky after which Malark placed the watermelon on his head. "*Fruit salad's requital craps melon on my head.*"

The crowd parted for Levitsky as he floated towards the wall. Putting his hands against the soggy concrete he lamented,

> Blatant, audiences, are their uneven gaps
> For, even their brave affinities are but pap

To those teeth most swollen, those bones above
heads
The Tectum's gob whose gappéd teeth we spread
For better or for worse—there is no clue
Through which Muslim, Christian, Mormon, or Jew
May claw curiosity and decipher staff
Decode this, Fibber, and merrily laugh.

A rumbling behind the wall crescendoed and then typewriters flooded onto Levitsky. Did he know this would happen? Did he have the second sight? The crowd gasped and the architect pushed through them all. He picked up a typewriter as though it were someone else's baby. "We better melt these down and make a giant helmet!" he advised.

From the mound of typewriters, Levitsky's hand appeared. Then his face and body clambered out in sequence. "What…did I do…to deserve this?"

"Too much," answered Fibber as he wiped the ale from his mouth and helped Levitsky. Yulia searched the room for a simultaneous avalanche. Was there another on its way?

Fibber held up a typewriter. "It's a boy!" Kicking a stool away from the table he dragged up a chair and parked his behind on the rickety rocking chair.

He plonked the typewriter down and acquainted himself with the writing machine and developed a strange kind of concentration.

Malark wiped watermelon from his hands and went to stand over Fibber. "What do you think *you're* doing?"

"Work. Please leave." His voice was flat and cold. But having failed to make an impression he raised his voice. "Everyone out! *That's an order from the Overseer!*"

The angry and confused guests dropped their tankards and bits of boiled meat and grumbled into the corridor outside where they returned to their floors.

Their murmuring and cursing pleased Fibber. "That's right. The evening is over," he said with grim satisfaction. "Go back to your respective floors. Don't come back."

"I'll go find Kosha," said Malark as he pointed toward the avalanche of typewriters. "He can melt these stupid things down."

Fibber pounded the table with his fist and then glared at his deputy. "It's ethically wrong to believe something without evidence," hissed Fibber. "Neither of us has evidence to support what we believe. I'm going to try and come up with some evidence...just for me...do you understand? As for getting rid of these things, you'll do no such thing."

"What do you want?" Malark tightened.

"*I want to work!*" shouted Fibber as he cleared the table of plates. "The party is over. Haven't you heard?" he yelled as he pointed to the exit.

Malark ignored Oksana as he got half-dressed and stormed out of the brothel. "I get all the legends," said Oksana as she and the other prostitutes prepared themselves for bed.

Yulia wrapped herself in a blanket and then watched over Fibber. "I suppose you want me to get ready for bed as well," she said with that resentful pity found in one-night stands.

Melting like butter, Fibber shook his head and then touched her hand gently. "Please stay…you are the only sane person here."

"Apart from you," said Yulia as she sat on the table.

"No." He started typing. "That is not what I said."

Levitsky shook off his anxiety about suffering through avalanches of typewriters and busied himself with putting out candles and looking for forgotten wallets amongst the mattresses strewn about the floor. "There will be words tonight… words give actions, but only when we're deaf," he whispered. He would sleep on a pile of hay in the corner and dream about long rivers whose waters turned red by setting suns.

The typing of Dante Fibber soothed the room. Listening for a while Yulia yawned and then fell asleep when Fibber smiled in her direction, looking for something.

DAY TWO

At sunrise light shot through the wasteland and the clearing heated. Flowers next to the thatched door uncurled and their pollen dispersed like sperm.

Inside the hovel Agapov was fast asleep in the corner, her tired body covered by an extra blanket. Lukum was awake and sitting at the wooden table. Under her breath, she muttered monologues, preparing herself for her reality.

"The truth gets you nowhere. It gets you buried," she said as acrid smoke from the stove swirled through the vent. "Where did it get King Midas? How different things were back then. Marsyas challenged Apollo to a music contest where he played an oboe and Apollo a lyre. When Apollo won, the condition was that Marsyas would be flogged—but one of the judges, King Midas, voted against Apollo and was punished forthwith and given the ears of a donkey."

She could hear the wind pattering the long grass outside.

"King Midas was ashamed of his ears and wore a cap to cover them," she whispered to herself. "He visited the barber one day and the man cutting his hair saw everything. Afterwards, the barber snuck off to the forest, dug a hole in the ground, and whispered into it everything he knew about the

King's donkey ears. He refilled the hole and thought he was hiding the secret. But then a shrub grew from the hole and its leaves whispered the truth about the King's ears to every passer-by and their dog. Soon everyone knew and King Midas drank bull's blood and killed himself. The truth gets you nowhere. It gets you buried. Apollo punished him too—"

The wind blew the thatched door open, which banged against its twiggy latches. Breezes flapped the sorry-looking interior and maps blew everywhere. Lukum stood up, walked outside, and sat cross-legged in the sand.

Urged awake by the wind, Agapov saw the dissident beyond the doorway. She wrapped herself in rags as smoke lashed the walls and made everything greasy black with a strange smell.

"Good morning," said Agapov as she slurped leftover grass soup. When there was no reply, she joined Lukum outside and inhaled the cold air.

"You are so young," offered Lukum.

"You'll catch your death sitting out here."

"I hope to catch it from you."

Agapov said, "I'm not going to kill you—I don't care what you say—"

"I have fed you and given you refuge and a place to sleep. But still, you refuse to kill me? Have no you understanding of good manners? You are so ungrateful. You will end up like Apollo."

"What happened to him?"

"Gods go nowhere. They live in eternity," replied Lukum plainly. "His chariot was drawn by griffins and carried bow and arrows. He turned his lover into a laurel tree and that tree is worshipped to this day. They built the Tectum on that tree. Its roots are blackheads in the face of the world. Apollo was the God of poetry, was he not?"

"Apollo deals in prophesies. What do you think your fate will be?"

The wind tussled her hair. "My destiny aligns with King Midas."

"It's a hassle to worry about people robbing you but there are worse fates," rendered Agapov.

Lukum's mass increased in proportion to her despair. "I am ashamed of my deformities. My body is normal and my soul is mutated," muttered the dissident quietly. "I look upon human beings with fondness whilst the other Bluebloods see naught but flesh and bone. They witness matter to be weighed. They do not even believe in ghosts."

Dead grass floated over her kneecaps and she hit them aggressively.

"How contaminated am I? Murdering my own soul every day I am a dictator in my own right. My dominion is one of grey tones and I look upon it with fondness…"

Agapov sighed. It was not a good start to the day.

Several miles away, a log cabin, a wooden shed, and a chicken pen sat alone on the scraggy wasteland. The farm was owned by the Zolotov family which consisted of Olga, Marina Zolotov, and their biological son, Melker.

Busy in the kitchen, Olga fed the stove with logs and brushed her hands free of wood. She had brown hair and piggy eyes that saw everything. Her body was wide and supported by strong legs crowned by metallic mud-caked boots. She wore a long Amish-style dress that covered everything but her hands and face. She seemed to be the essence of temperance.

Her sleepy son, Melker, wandered into the kitchen and stood next to the table. "Good morning, dear," said Olga.

"I dreamed of risotto and lamb's kidneys," replied Melker. "The kidneys were soaked in milk because it was October." He remembered his chores. "I'll do the chickens..."

"Hot and sour squid with lime juice, sherry, honey, and ginger," teased Olga. "You deep fry them and then drizzle the marinade over them. That was my dream about Japan—" Her words were punctuated by the sound of wood splitting in the stove.

Melker yawned and donned his winter coat.

The chickens were ravenous when he discovered them. Brushing seed powder from his hands he realized his palms were tough. "We can't be like painters, can we?" he sighed as he squelched into the shed. There were pigs inside and they squealed with excitement as he poured out a bucket of leftovers. He topped up the piggy stove, discerned happy snorts and shuffling, and returned quickly to the house because it was cold.

Back in the house, the other mother, Marina, peeled potatoes at the table. She had short red hair, bags under her eyes, and pendulous ears that defined her face. She wore a loud shawl over her dress and her boots were cleaner than those belonging to her family members. Her hands were fat and she flicked one side of her nose as she regarded her son when he removed his winter coat.

"I assume you'll want to write today?" she said with common annoyance.

He nodded dimly and tried to turn his attention to the floorboards.

"You do the laundry first," said Marina as she plopped a naked potato in a bowl.

"But that will take half the day!"

"Then you will write in the other half." She liked to think the potatoes were people. "You'll be glad to know the pigs will be nearby."

"That's right. I have to do the pigs and clean the chicken coop," said Melker.

Another naked potato plopped into the bowl. "You could have done that already instead of lecturing me. You are like that pork stew with saffron rice you made the other night. The rice was like steel," scorned his mother. "And if you think I am trying to keep you from writing—you are spot on—"

"Marina," snapped the other mother.

"How could *anyone* sanction that propaganda you write?" She ignored her wife who stared angrily at the philistine she had married. "Written with the Blueblood Seal, indeed. They might be novels and short stories. But what happened to all that bad publicity we used to have? I have to find my own son writing propaganda. You have become a character reference."

"They are only propaganda if you read them as such. Is there anyone free from the occasional crime of creating propaganda?" asked Melker.

"Mine neither kills people nor belittles the working woman," replied Marina.

Olga sighed over the sink and tapped her fingers on the counter.

"The stories I tell are the only ones the state allows me to tell. Is there any shortage of stories in histories and battles? What do you know?" rallied Melker. "Every inch of spare time I have is spent earning food from the state…but I never write what they feel…only what I feel."

"Who would have thought that I would raise a lunatic?" said Marina as she deprived another potato of its skin. "We are having chicken marengo tonight and there's nothing you can do about it. You're going to kill me a chicken. And will you kindly do the laundry?"

Olga volunteered, "I'll do the laundry. I have enough to do already. But I have no other commitments."

Eyeing the sorry-looking onions hanging from the ceiling, Marina sniggered and dried her hands. "The Spanish onions are milder than our English onions. That was a good year when our provisions came through—I would give my right hand for a Spanish onion."

"It can be arranged." Olga clomped out of the kitchen.

Melker remained for Marina's eulogy.

"There's more weevils than flour in this thing." Dragging a bucket towards her Marina discerned the tiny creatures making their society in the brown flour. "They are going to be our month's supply of protein," she said as she turned to Melker. "Don't forget that chicken. It'll be an hour's preparation for the one I have in mind…make sure you dispatch the right chicken…after you have finished doing the laundry. But that was abandoned…your mother has taken that over. In that case, you have hours to scribble your propaganda before that chicken meets its maker. Don't set your mind to it before the time comes. Otherwise, you can't go through with the culling. On the other hand, it might be where *stories* come from…"

Donning his winter coat Melker stormed out. In the hallway, he met a trunk and dragged it outside, across the yard, into the shed where the pigs watched him closely.

Shuffling into his writing bunker he opened the trunk and lifted out stacks of paper tied together with brown fingers of unwinding string. The stacks were numbered and he pulled out the most recent one. Removing the sheet scrawled with yesterday's words Melker started working:

Admiral Chervez thought ~~long and hard~~ about his attack plan. Across the ballroom, through bodies rotating to the brass band's belches, there stood the object of the admiral's love. Princess Winchester, recently widowed and touching the back of her hand with a greetings card she'd received from Admiral Chervez the day before. Her eyes shot through the moving bodies. She made out the well-groomed hair through happy heads ~~that were~~ heaving to and fro. She ~~frowned~~ smiled.

No matter the class from which the story had sprung, his story had something that glued the reader. Would the

Ministry for Culture enjoy the exploits of Admiral Chervez? What drove Melker to such distraction? He thought about the chicken…

In the covered wagon, the Maestro and the Bearded Lady snoozed awkwardly on wooden boards. Their bodies were twisted like statues in some provincial gallery presenting the past. The Chicken Boy was sleeping peacefully and kicked his orange legs when something startled him. Was there someone outside? Had *they* come for him? And who were *they* anyway? Listening to the bottles being tossed at the covered wagon, the Chicken Boy muttered an inquisitive "BOGACK?" He flexed his luminous talons and prayed using foreign words.

The Maestro had a dream where he was told people that their gold would be safe with him. He smiled to himself—but was shaken awake by the Chicken Boy clucking hysterically.

Another bottle smashed itself against the wagon's hull and sent the Chicken Boy running in circles. "BOGACK," screamed the Chicken Boy. "BOGACK!"

When the Maestro sat up, he whacked his forehead against a cauldron of soup. He pointed an accusatory finger at the sleeping Bearded Lady. "Listen to me you androgynous goon—don't put the soup there! What have I told you about cause and effect?"

"No pesos…muy picante…" murmured the Bearded Lady who ignored everything and fell back into a dream that featured a cute bartender, a cactus, and the Old Testament.

The Maestro reached helplessly at the furious clucking Chicken Boy. "What's wrong, my darling?" He looked to the door and turned red. "Who the hell is throwing bottles outside?

"BOGACK!"

"You've nothing to worry about as you won't be in *Othello*. I would never let you near that dangerous material—" Another bottle struck the wagon. "The Strongman and his pipe weed. He probably washed it down with beer..."

He rolled off of the wooden plank and yanked on his perfumed boots. He opened the door and went to take a step down only to jam his foot into a dwarf's mouth. The two bodies dropped onto the ground where they moaned and swore at one another. The Maestro checked his ankles to make sure his feet were still attached. Honza stuck his hand in his mouth, counted his teeth, and gave the Maestro a hard look. "What the hell is wrong with you?"

"Who said that?" asked the Maestro as he looked around. "Mother, is that you?"

"*My damn teeth*—"

The Maestro looked down. "Oh." He creased his mouth. "You were the one throwing bottles?"

"I was trying to wake you, you mother."

From behind the covered wagon, the Strongman and the Astrologer appeared carrying their boots as weapons. "What's all the commotion?" asked the Astrologer. Then she lowered her eyeline. "Oh..."

"You work for this jackass?" asked Honza as he pointed at the Maestro.

The Strongman stifled a laugh. The Astrologer answered, "I'm afraid we do, yes."

"*I'm afraid that we do*," mimicked the Maestro. "I am afraid that you were unemployable when I found you in the countryside. I whipped you into shape and made you employable."

Honza raised an eyebrow.

"Not literally, you have to understand. I metaphorically whipped her into shape," soothed the Maestro.

"What did the other mummies say?" asked Honza.

"What?"

"When you survived having your brain removed—*what did the other mummies say?*"

The Strongman laughed, unzipped his trousers, and whipped out his penis. "This one has spirit!" he announced as the crushing humiliation set into his criminally under-rated groin.

Averting her eyes, the Astrologer coughed: "This one has Alzheimer's."

"He is going to have my boot up his backside," promised the Maestro.

"Light travels faster than sound," said Honza who had seen worse things with Agapov.

"And...?"

"You were pretty bright before you opened your mouth."

Everybody laughed at the Maestro. The Bearded Lady stood in the wagon's doorway and pointed and laughed as the Maestro curled into a soggy ball of resentment.

The Astrologer knelt down. "What is your name?"

"My name's Honza. I'm from Detroit," said the dwarf.

"You are a long way from home, Honza."

"Not as far as your father was when you were conceived—"

"Maestro—give the man a job!" laughed the Strongman.

"Give me a job…or else." Honza smiled.

Staring down at the new recruit, the Maestro folded his arms and harumphed. "Let's get something straight… I'm the boss around here—" The Chicken Boy shot over the Bearded Lady's shoulder and sent the Maestro careening onto the ground where he tumbled forward.

Using the Chicken Boy's neck, Honza swung himself onto the Chicken Boy's back and rode him around the perimeter of the room leaving a cloud of dust wherever they went.

"It's a sign!" said the Strongman as he stepped on the Maestro's back.

"Put him on at half-time," advised the Astrologer.

Standing with difficulty and hating everyone, the Maestro joined the Bearded Lady. "How long do you give him?" asked the Bearded Lady.

"We'll have to put him in *Othello*," said the Maestro in a grave voice.

"If she will stir hither, I shall seem to notify unto her—I would rather die than see him as Bianca."

"In happy time, Iago."

"A brave casting," warned the Bearded Lady. "Iago needs to be less brittle. We may want Honza to bleed to death by that point anyway."

"Roderigo?" Pausing the Maestro's lip curled. "Too naïve."

"Most heathenish and most gross."

"I don't think Honza could ever be a father. Which means Cassio's out."

"Brabantio? I suppose that would be against the rules of nature—" Then horror came over the Bearded Lady's face. "You can't be serious…"

"Honza will have done the state some service. We ought to remember him as he was," said the Maestro as he fawned over the dubious casting that stained his mind.

The Bearded Lady was taken aback, "He can't play Othello!"

"Well, that's what happens when you make fun of me."

"If you want to punish him, make him play Desdemona!"

Turning on his deputy manager, the Maestro hissed, "For an ex-woman you're bitter."

"If you keep talking that way, you're going to be an ex-man," the Bearded Lady said as blew out his cheeks with a puff of disappointed air. "Where the hell is this Overseer, anyway?"

Watching the Chicken Boy sprinting around the room's perimeter, the Maestro chuckled. "Fibber and Malark are probably in the brothel. Or burning the midnight lamp and doing paperwork—they'll be sleeping it off. That crap has kept people up since they invented banks. They can't accept how all their poems and paintings amount to jack squat," spat the Maestro.

In the background, the Strongman waved. "I knew Jack Squat. He was a good man!"

The Maestro clicked his heels together like the Fascist he was. "Maybe *Othello* isn't such a bad idea. It's a good play to cast when you have enemies."

"Where do you get this shit?" said the Bearded Lady in a flurry of frankness. "I'll be far away from here when I die," he promised.

Cupping his hands, the Maestro recovered control: "Othello! Get off my Chicken Boy!"

In the brothel, flies swarmed around rotting vegetables and the boiled meat had hardened overnight. Fibber had worked the night through, writing pages of material, and as he typed the last word, Yulia moaned awake and stared crack-eyed at him. "Good morning," she said.

"Good night," replied Fibber tiredly.

Lifting her head, she rubbed the back of her neck. "It's too late for that."

"Time isn't real. But thank you for staying."

"You're the one who stayed." She eyed the ceiling. "Your quarters are upstairs."

Sucking the festering remains from a dirty mug, Fibber spat out the liquid and cleared his throat. "What's going through your head?"

Yulia smirked and snorted loudly. "We know about the fall from Christian theology but the idea starts with the Platonic tradition. Mankind has descended from a spiritual existence to a material one and the guilt we have today comes from transgressions during an earlier life," she said as she stood up and grabbed a nearby chair and pulled it next to Fibber's stool. "For example, Eve and Adam have naught but unemployment and pain. Our guilt never belongs to us because every problem stems from Adam—and because of him, each of us deserves to be punished. On the other hand, some would say it's just symbols."

"What do you say?" asked Fibber.

"Nothing oral—one ought to be realistic."

The architect croaked awake underneath the table. "It's Friday," he said as he tapped his kneecaps to make sure they were still there. "I want you to thank Adam for my helmet."

"You must have read my *Othello* while I slept," Fibber told Yulia. "Which means I must have slept…"

There was a knock at the door and Fibber stood up swigging another glass of *something*. As he spat out the contents onto someone's back, he tripped on an ancient prostitute's leg. Regaining his balance, he wiped his beard, and opened the door.

Marshall Volkov was standing in the doorway and he had several thick layers of melted blue cheese tainting his long beard. He was wearing a bright red hard hat with straps that connected under his receding chin. His hair was mostly grey and he wore thick glasses which magnified his baleful eyes five times over. He wore golden overalls and dark black boots that glistened with polish and smelled terrible.

He wanted to introduce himself as the President of the Furnace Union. But he liked proving that every man, woman, and child needed conditioning which only he could provide.

"Today's work starts," stammered Fibber, "when the world catches fish. Goodbye."

Fibber tried to shut the door but Volkov jammed his boot into the gap.

"Do you know my name?" asked Volkov as he estimated the age of the cheese.

"You are the Dutch mathematician, Snell. I would love to talk about your new recipe for π but I have moved on to the cake. Goodbye," said Fibber again.

Kicking the door open, Volkov thumped inside and slammed the door behind him. "I didn't think that I would find you in a den of egregiousness," he began, "my sincerest hope that you are never sent the bill for this place. You would, no doubt, suffer a heart attack and die…"

"I should be so lucky."

"My name is Marshall Volkov. I am the official liaison between the furnace folk and the people whom their toil benefits. It was brought to my attention, therefore, that you insulted the foreman."

"I barely spoke to the twerp. It's my deputy you should scold—not me…"

"Putting to one side the influence of social democracy," interrupted Volkov as he adjusted his glasses and prepared himself for a speech of great length, "workers perform no conscious activity. We know this because Lenin taught us these things. You are responsible, therefore, for this deputy and everything he does."

"I used to be a writer," replied Fibber, "and Lenin wrote bad prose."

Malark appeared from behind a Turkish carpet and covered his ears using his hands. "Lenin, Lenin, Lenin—I don't need that word buzzing around my head in the morning. What on earth is wrong with you people?"

"You must be this so-called deputy. You seem to have forgotten your position. You're a worker and you're going to like it." Volkov pointed to the vomit stains on Malark's chest.

"It's too early to throw contradictions around inside a brothel," yawned Fibber.

"You'll wake everyone up with your nonsense," said Malark as some of the prostitutes shuffled into conscious activity, scavenging for liquid, and giving the men dyspeptic gazes.

Volkov gathered Fibber and Malark like two thin-shelled eggs from under a chicken. "The point is that you have abused the furnace workers," hissed Volkov.

"Change the charge and the accused," accused Fibber. "I think you're just a little man."

"It's perfectly natural to assume that a revolution is going to occur inside the Tectum. But it's gathering rather quicker than I would have imagined. We must avoid the Russian approach," said Volkov as he covered his eyes and raised his receding chin. "Mr. Fibber, can you put on some clothes?"

Fibber smiled at the slowly emerging employees of the brothel. "You see, girls?"

Malark squinted. "What's the difference between a pickpocket and a peeping tom? One snatches your watch, whilst the other watches your sna—"

"Thank you, deputy," interrupted Volkov.

"I'd like to paint you nude, Mr. President."

"Why don't we write an erotic novel instead?" said Fibber as he fumbled his testicles. "We could call it *When Volkov's Trousers Tightened*—I could add the stuff I wrote last night."

"Don't bother," said Yulia as she dried Fibber's trousers over an open fire.

"I shall make my report to Minister Jozlov," said Volkov as Fibber put his finger to his chapped lips, dragged Marshall Volkov under his arm, and raised his eyebrows.

"The minister doesn't care about our politics. If she had, she would have married you." He kissed Volkov's nose and ignored the taste of cheese. "I'm worried that if this place becomes a Communist paradise, then Lenin will be absolved of his sins. I won't allow that to happen. If things go the other way and we become monsters then the only punishment worthy of Lenin will be dementia."

Volkov wriggled and listened uneasily. "You're an anarchist."

Yulia sauntered over rubbing her eyes. "He's not just a romantic," she cut in. "You should define your terms before you start slinging mud. He's a *conservative anarchist.*" Tugging on Volkov's beard she whipped her hand free of cheese. "If you have any interest in self-interest then you should read La Rouchefoucauld. His pride is equal to your honesty." She laughed and clapped her hands. "You're as clear on the subject of egoism as he ever was!"

Peering through her partition, Oksana spied the interlocutors and snarled at the group.

"I have as much hope as a freedom fighter in a Tsarist court," thought Volkov. He forced his thick glasses back onto his face. "I'll move to my second point of order," he restarted. "There is a terrorist in the Tectum—What are you going to do about it?"

"I don't sleep with terrorists *or* freedom fighters," replied Yulia calmly.

"My good woman—I wasn't asking you," replied Volkov.

In the background, Oksana granted a mirthless chuckle. "There's no freedom to be fought over," she estimated pessimistically.

Volkov smiled. "Those are my sentiments *exactly* young lady!" Repulsed by what she saw, Oksana closed the partition and Volkov turned to Fibber. "Comrade…the going rate…"

"Wait!" shouted Fibber as he grabbed the man's shoulders. "There's a terrorist? With bombs?"

Meanwhile, Malark cleared the table with his hand and wondered why he was naked.

Fibber twitched and pointed to Malark. "It's not *him*—is it?"

"I don't want to destroy things—I want to paint," said Malark as he smelled his fingers. "If I burn the canvas, it is because the painting wasn't good enough and artists did the same for centuries." He looked around the room. "Where are my clothes, Oksana?"

"Im Ofen," replied her voice behind the partition.

"My day improves, Mr. President." He looked at Volkov who had wetted his trousers. "Why are you the only person wearing clothes? I love your glasses—they make you look smart." Marshall Volkov was worried for his life and he decided to cook breakfast for everyone, discuss his plans for revolution, and help the brothel committee find clothes for Malark to wear.

Agapov was not having a good day. Plum Lukum forced her inside the hovel because the occasional patrol would pay her a visit and they were not people she could afford to aggravate. "You'll need to hide me," said Agapov bluntly. "I'm not going back out there…"

"You are more use to me here. You will fix my ego ideal: my basket of positive ideals and the things I would like to accomplish."

"You told me how you tried to do that. What could you *possibly* do now apart from keeping your mouth shut?" reasoned Agapov.

Her entire body shook with rage. "Revolt," she hissed. "Pillage. Murder…I could kill them for what they did to me…but that would be too easy…I require a rounder revenge."

She stood under the vent and looked through it at the cloudy skies outside. "The Creator Goddess of the Bella Coola people killed the giants who once populated the world," explained Lukum. "She built mountains from their bodies and made the world in her image. I must think of the future because the past has no time…but…what is that noise…?"

In the clearing outside a raid tank squelched to a halt. These monstrous machines were as feared as the soldiers they carried. The hatch opened and two men appeared. The first man was called Captain Gurkin and he was wearing brass armour and knuckle-dusters with glass. His scissor-clipped hair was packed under a dull grey cap and the shining duckbill cast a shadow over his thinning eyebrows and his bright green eyes. He had a very small mouth and his hands had tufts of hair on their knuckles. He was carrying an official document in his right hand that had been rolled into a tube and fastened tight using a string made from human hair. The second man was called Private Rakovsky and he was wearing military-green overalls and something like a white naval cap that had left his eyebrows to the mercies of the elements. His arms were thick with muscle, his legs were almost bursting through his overall legs, and his barrel chest cast a shadow on the constituents of the sandy clearing. Both marched towards the thatched door but it was Gurkin who kicked the door in.

"Good morning," said Gurkin. "Captain Gurkin and Private Rakovsky reporting for duty. It is noted that Rakovsky opened the door when the resident refused to co-operate."

Rakovsky frowned.

"You are not permitted guests," he reminded Lukum as he swivelled toward Agapov. "Who are you?"

"This woman rescued me from the storm." Agapov swallowed.

"You speak as though the prisoner were in a position to help. What is your name?"

"Madam Marielle Agapov."

"The order was issued yesterday. I do not have the energy to determine whether you are confident or stupid. Private, remove this woman from the prisoner's presence—"

"I told her everything!" shouted Lukum. "The Bluebloods and their smearing campaign. The nature of the Tectum—"

"If Emmanuel Mounier analysed Lukum, he would find that she was shallow, egocentric, inauthentic, and materialistic. You share neither values nor dogmas with anyone. You are without vocation and cannot be divided—not in the absence of a large knife, anyway."

Private Rakovsky raised his hand, stepped forward, and politely interrupted the conversation. "I think I have located the problem with the indiscernibility of identicals. There is no evidence to suggest that you're any different from this woman. Therefore, what property belongs to her must also belong to you; and what property belongs to you must also belong to her. This may extend to emotional properties and sensations when reading Rilke and—"

Gurkin flicked his wrist and his knuckle dusters cascaded across Rakovsky's cheek.

"I must apologize for my deputy," said Gurkin as Rakovsky rubbed his cheek. "Rakovsky is one of those new *cultured soldiers*. His job is to absorb the very same filth produced by artist-scum. He will have made himself familiar, for example, with the Fibber's poetry and Malark's paintings." He gave Rakovsky a stern look and the private marched out. Gurkin spoke quietly. "Enough pretend, Lukum. I require some advice."

Agapov stood between them. "She won't help you!"

"Be quiet—and sit down," replied Gurkin as Agapov took a seat at the rickety table.

"Gurkin belongs to the Tectum," sneered Lukum.

"Tell me about Angeloff," instructed Gurkin as he wiped his knuckle duster.

"A planner of bombings who targeted my jurisdiction on more than one occasion. He enjoyed destroying public transport."

"I must inform you that Angeloff is in the Tectum. Not being a man who benefits experiments he must be *dealt* with."

Swallowing her regret, she stared down Captain Gurkin. "It's purpose?" she began. "What are you doing with those people?"

"The meek shall inherit the earth. We never think of that as a conditional," he replied.

"Because it's a certainty."

"The conditions under which the meek shall inherit the earth are tempestuous at best." He narrowed his eyes, licked his lips, and sighed. "Why are you smiling?"

Lukum said nothing and then listened to the wind getting sucked through the vent.

"I followed orders, Lukum—I did then and I do now," assured Gurkin.

"The goose-God will ensure that my fate is just."

He sniggered. "You and your Gods—who rot the world…"

"What are you going to do with Angeloff?" asked Lukum professionally.

"We expect that the Overseer will perform his duties. If this fails to occur then our independent variable shall have to visit the Tectum sooner than we expected." Gripped by something in the air, he twisted his small mouth, drew a small breath, and recited poetry.

Then suffer shall the meek bones
And praised will the unenlightened be
Morning dew, copper stones
And echoes of the ancient ash tree.

Straightening his spine, Gurkin tapped his ceremonial armour, and marched outside where he ordered Rakovsky to conceal his book of poetry. Once inside the raid tank, they chugged across the landscape where they would visit another dissident. But first a spot of lunch—Rakovsky abandoned his sandwich halfway through, remembering the ecstasy of Rilke, and began to describe the landscape in lyrically intense verse.

Meanwhile, Gurkin plotted his next move as he simmered over his coffee. The events that would transpire would have to be executed both metaphorically and literally.

Draping laundry on the line outside, Olga watched Marina's skirt slashing through the mud. She materialized between the sheets as the wind picked up and she watched her wife. Olga picked up another shirt, draped it on the line, and cracked her knuckles. "Why do you encourage him?" asked Marina.

"He's our son." Olga arranged a quilt on the line. "One ought to encourage children," she added as she looked at the sky. "Do you think this sun will keep up?"

"Not what he's doing, surely? What Melker is doing is morally bankrupt—"

"The fact that he's our son is plain to see. Why don't you get our sperm donor here?" She scoffed and flicked a towel free of liquid. "The Bluebloods admire Melker and they will fund him with provisions as long as we fund him with love."

"You want his fruits," hissed Marina. "The stuff he gets for writing that rubbish—"

"Don't pretend that we don't share in those fruits. Melker wouldn't know what to say if he heard you say that," replied Olga.

"I seriously doubt that."

"Not many read his books. Besides, who can read these days? The Bluebloods buy a copy and pass it around to their friends. But that's not deplorable—it's just the nature of the industry." She pointed at her wife. "He gets better than extra fuel and food...we get security and safety because of our son...safety from patrols and sordid visits."

The chickens that they purchased came in wooden cages held together with brown string matted with oil. Pulling one over, Marina sat on one and the chicken inside glared at her.

"You talk about the nature of the industry. You ought to become an agent," muttered Olga. "You could sell mountains of propaganda and we could have provisions *that* way."

Dragging the quilt down the line, Olga squinted. "You have promised to teach me how to read—"

"How did he learn without me?" She pondered. "We want books and reading to be positive things. But why?"

"You are the exception to your own rule. Help me with this—"

They each took an end of the duvet, yanked at both ends, and made it taut, then tossed the duvet over the line. Olga poked momentarily from below while Marina pulled at corners.

"I worry about him sitting in there. He suffers for his art," proffered Olga.

"There was a time when we ate smoked haddock. We eke out the evenings chewing potatoes and chicken and the infrequent hog. Maybe I made the wrong choice to leave my life in the city."

"That was not living," said Olga as she picked up the laundry basket and returned inside.

In the covered wagon the Bearded Lady tried his best to ignore the sounds outside. He opened his eyes and found a copy of *Othello* hanging from the ceiling by a solitary string. Then he shut his eyes again, laid back, and composed some verse.

Sordid floors beneath your feet
Do oft breed melancholy castes
But ranks falsely compete
As two hundred ropes to one mast
For, when in anguish, do states
Breathlessly topple into late
Those blithe men and women
Release teeth and do tall tales relate.

"Rehearsal!" exclaimed the Maestro outside. "I have found my Iago!"

The Bearded Lady prepared himself and then ventured outside. He saw piles of typewriters everywhere. Where had these peculiar things come from? The Chicken Boy typed on one. Transfixed by the writing process, he behaved peculiarly and said nothing. Why was this happening? A less peculiar sight was Honza typing and swearing in equal measure at the flapping pages of his script. The Bearded Lady looked despairingly at the Astrologer and the Strongman who were building the stage. They hammered, sawed, and sucked their fingers when it went wrong.

There were three men wearing monk's habits, moreover, who were as yet unknown to the Bearded Lady and the rest of The Metaphysical Circus. The monks were engaged in prayer until the Maestro shouted, "Our beloved Bearded Lady has surfaced from the cave of sleep!"

Bugger, thought the Bearded Lady.

"He may be a little goofy in the head because of those hormones the good doctor gave him but he's a solid man," confirmed the Maestro.

One of the habited men scuttled over and addressed the Maestro with a side-eye directed at the Bearded Lady. He had a sharp nose, thin lips, and freckled cheeks. "I may be a stickler for the rejection of past authorities and preconceived opinions," said Drast, "but a Bearded Lady who has undergone a gender re-assignment surgery is no longer a Bearded Lady. The novelty has been removed by force."

Then another habited man came over. He was thinner than the other one. He had thick lips, a button nose, and sarcastic eyes that laughed at the world. "Given how science is a unified system based upon metaphysical foundations," said Pommel, "we can but view the *bearded-lady-man* in the knowledge that God implanted this change and thus guarantees the change." He blinked satisfactorily and looked at the Bearded Lady who sucked his teeth at the objectification that had encouraged the sex-change in the first place.

"I'm enjoying the philosophical dung-throwing competition," replied the Bearded Lady, "but what are you doing here? I can only assume that one of you will be our Iago."

"*Your* Iago?" parodied Drast as he picked his toenails. "I suppose God is happy implanting arrogance to boot."

"It's so like you to turn my ideas against yourself," said Pommel.

"These trouser strains dropped off the typewriters," interrupted the Maestro. "Iago has his mind on bigger things." He gestured towards the third habited man who was sitting cross-legged on the other side of the Fourth Floor.

The third man was completely silent. He had large feet packaged in sandals and his hairy legs crept out from under the habit. His eyes were solemn and grey and his mouth was a permanent straight line of observed silence. A small curl of black hair descended over his forehead and he stared dully ahead—but that's not to say he was unaware of his surroundings.

"His name is Angeloff," added the Maestro with a flourish of the hand. "They are freedom fighters from the city. That is why we get on so well," approved the Maestro.

The Bearded Lady was unimpressed. "Can he speak?"

"Of course, he can speak! But if wisdom takes the form of silence, then I can only pray that you take some notes!"

You will die, thought the Bearded Lady.

Kneeling by his leader Drast, rubbed his hands to warm them up. "You need rest, silence, and patient meditation. Your acolytes will aid you in this…" He waved at Pommel and the latter came over and they lifted Angeloff into the air. Bringing him several metres hence they plopped him onto a pre-ordained pillow. They then took turns reading aloud from *Othello*.

Meanwhile, the Strongman and the Astrologer took a break from their carpentry. In what would prove to be hopelessly deluded hope, they believed that the stage would benefit the play.

"I'm going to give our Maestro this hammer. I'm going to teach him how to beat himself to death," gasped the Strongman.

"Did you know that kleptolagnia is when you get sexually aroused by theft?" vented the Astrologer.

"Are you saying I should give it a try? I've used up all the other kinds of arousal—"

"Drast and Pommel were sweaty and promiscuous when they first appeared with Angeloff and those typewriters…"

"You mean they stole Angeloff?"

"Maybe they do that every day to arouse themselves. It's their last chance for erection."

"I'm trying to wean the Maestro off bestiality," announced the Strongman.

"Proof?" Her eyes welled up when no answer came. "The Chicken Boy's fair game?"

"I swore to withhold the truth," replied the Strongman as he crossed his huge heart, "though I can't stand the man."

Casting her eye towards the Chicken Boy the Astrologer noticed he was prodding a typewriter using his feathery fingers. "Look at him," she said. "He's been typing for an hour."

The Strongman smirked and coughed. "Do you think he's jailbait?"

Smacking his bicep, the Astrologer descended the staircase that they had built and walked over to the Chicken Boy where she looked over his feathery shoulder. "What are you typing there, little one?"

"Bogack." His voice was sober and bellowed the cold reverence of propositions.

"I see…" She pointed to the words that he had typed on the page. "What's this here?"

"*Feel*."

"Well, isn't that—" Turning white the sound of shattering glass stabbed her mind. "Did you—you—you didn't say bogack—you—"

"*Feel*," repeated the Chicken Boy as he reverently continued typing.

"Oh—God." Backing off the Astrologer feigned normality. "Carry on, little one," she stammered as her frightened feet carried her to Honza who had been typing and swearing.

Honza finished typing, folded his arms, and shook his head in disdain.

"Honza," began the Astrologer carefully, "how are you doing? Feel any different?"

The Astrologer was quickly reassured that he was the same when Honza explained that he was "pissed off" with the typewriter: "You can't type shit on this. The keys are bricks." He looked at her. "What are you staring at? What the hell do *you* want?"

"Well, I—"

"You looked scared as shit, girl." He spoke carefully. "What's wrong with you?"

"What are you writing?"

"Just these stupid lines," he said. "Othello talks too much. If he just shut the hell up none of this dumb shit would've happened to him. He kills his wife and keeps on talking—*I got this heavenly sight, blow smoke up my ass and roast it, Desdemona*—Desde-who-*gives*-a-goddamn? No wonder the mother-fucka kills himself…"

"What a prognostic," chortled the Astrologer. "Are those direct quotations?"

"If they were I'd quit my day job and be an angel." Honza sucked his teeth.

Downstairs Marshall Volkov and Fibber visited the second floor. Unbeknownst to them the man that they had come to find was busy being prepared to appear in *Othello* on the fourth floor. On the second floor was where chefs and publicans had gathered. Meanwhile, green grocers and butchers had lined the "streets" with their stalls. Crates, produce and butchered animals hung from the ceiling on swinging steel chains.

Volkov muttered, "Shall we test Angeloff with bayonets?"

"I would rather test this circus man," replied Fibber as the two men walked past the stalls. "We're meant to be putting on *Othello* together. We have to entertain the residents. But *Othello* is too short for any lasting anaesthesia. *King Lear* or *Hamlet* is better suited to the kind of anaesthesia that we're after…"

"Or the Scottish play. That's long and good," proffered Volkov.

"True," half-agreed Fibber. "Who was your informant?"

"A good bastard doesn't reveal his weasel's passport—not unless the time is ripe and fruit starts falling." Volkov guided them into a manufactured alleyway.

"Oh no," said Fibber when he saw the stall.

"I'm sure that Lenin looked the same when his contemporaries thought about the meaning of life," commented Volkov. "Notwithstanding, we should make our meaning in collective forms. Take the furnace union, for example. They suffer no turbulence down there and yet we think that rapid social change requires turbulence—or is somehow born out of it."

Novikoff strutted beyond the borders of her stall. "Overseer! You have come for my pistachios! I told you they were good. Have you changed your position on my daughter?" She paused and laughed. "You would have to be with her to do that! Ha-ha! But I don't suppose that you've changed your views on adoption, Overseer?"

Simmering, Fibber poked Volkov in the chest. "Stay *here*, Volkov." Then he followed Novikoff into the stall and was enveloped by darkness and numerous barrels of pistachios.

He found one barrel using his hands and took a deep breath. He plunged his head into the mound of pistachios and when he removed his head his face was powdered. Blowing pistachio powder from his chapped lips he noticed Novikoff edging towards him.

"Overseer," called Novikoff from the dark. "You look tired—I think you may have been having too much fun with those hussies. I suggest you find yourself a partner and settle down with some hogs and chickens. As wind batters the windows you can dream about that time when you ran the Tectum with an iron fist…"

Fibber dunked his head back into the pistachios but Novikoff grabbed his shoulders and threw him onto the ground.

Ruffling his kinky hair, the Overseer viewed Novikoff towering over him.

"I've not had sex in years; that's too long for a woman like me," declared Novikoff. "I've gone mad. Do you think women are averse to sex? You don't think women *enjoy* sex?" She licked her lips and ran her hands down her sides. "I must inform you that when fields are barren, we women become hungry. What is to be done? If we seek out our carnal pleasures, we are called whores and hussies and men (and women) think we're no better than those hussies on the lower level."

Fibber coughed.

"We're none of us here for *humane* reasons. You have more sperm than words," announced Novikoff solemnly. "But you spray it in the wrong direction. My husband had better aim and he fathered my daughter. The plague destroyed him and I ended up here. Do you want to know *why* I was directed towards the Tectum?"

"Spit it out, woman!"

Spitting out two pistachio shells Novikoff grinned in the half-shadow. "The government wished to punish me for molestation: a molester by temperament and vocation. More to the point I want you more than life itself. I want you with me…on me…what you will—"

"Lie with you? On you?" spluttered Fibber. "There may be nothing whatsoever which condemns your words—but I have found love with Yulia!"

"The hussy?"

Fibber coughed again. "I don't think of her as a prostitute. She's a woman and I've fallen in love with her and that's the end of the matter. I don't consider myself an adulterer. But why am I trembling?" He moaned as though he had stubbed his toe.

"You want me…*say it, pig*…"

His boots scraped against broken shells as he tried to scramble away from her embrace. "Nature would not allow this without some instruction," hissed Fibber bluntly. "Your nose…your ears…your lips, your…*pistachios*. Who cares if the Devil is here!"

Noticing his weakness, Novikoff fell onto Fibber and the two began copulating.

Waiting patiently outside Volkov mulled over his profound sense of history and how that history constituted an inevitable truth. Suddenly the ceiling broke and plummeted twenty typewriters onto his body and he was crushed instantly. A collective scream filled the second floor as butchers, bakers, cooks, and waiters rushed over to witness the mangled remains of the President of the Furnace Union.

The moment Marshall Volkov was crushed, however, Fibber and Novikoff achieved orgasm simultaneously and lay in their powdery bed of humiliation and degradation. Hearing the screams outside they jumped up, dressed themselves, and then ran outside where they found butchers, grocers, and publicans fighting over typewriters. Possessed by an uncontrollable desire to write, these people fought one another for writing implements, thought Fibber as he noticed a cheese-stained hand poking limply out of the melange of rubble and typewriters…

In the wasteland, sharp rain was heavy. Cutting grass for their follow-up soup, Plum Lukum spotted Captain Gurkin's raid tank bumbling along the horizon. She dropped her dagger and ran after the machine in the hope that she would somehow claim her death and find peace. Chasing after her was Marielle Agapov who trailed her hostess for one mile before she caught up with her. She reached for her costumed talons and failed to slow the surprisingly fit pensioner.

"Come back!" shouted Lukum as she gulped the tank's exhaust fumes. "I want you to kill me! You cannot be short of ammo after you melted down my buses—I want you to shoot those buses into my body! We have an old tradition of target practice in this country! Use my frame!"

Enduring the exhaust fumes, Agapov gasped for air. "I need you to make more grass soup. He's got better things to do than kill you," she promised.

The hatch on the raid tank opened and Captain Gurkin popped up and sneered down. "Wake up and accept your fate. You've got no friends remaining," he gloated as his body gyrated. "Go into the city and they'll treat you like the Belgian terrorist you truly are!"

"You are lying to me—you would not dare!" yelled Lukum over the exhaust pipes.

"What they don't know can't hurt them," came the reply as the raid tank chugged ceaselessly forward. "I'll be in touch when I need more information," Gurkin said as he returned inside, shut the hatch, and sat next to his lieutenant. Private Rakovsky changed into fifth gear and persuaded the accelerator as he dropped his collection of Emily Dickinson poetry.

The raid tank left the two women gagging as the machine chugged into the distance at increased speed. The oppressive fumes forced them to the ground and together they waited for the air to clean. "Foiled again. This happens every week," grumbled Lukum as she beat the ground. "To hell with the man and his stupid hat," she protested.

"It's going to snow. We need to get back to your hovel—"

"Hovel! What a word! I lived in a private mansion in the parliamentary district," she reminisced and burst into tears. "I spend my time wanting to freeze."

Snow fell and coated the wasteland like something magical. She pulled Lukum away and they walked back to the sandy clearing where the hovel sat like an irritable crab.

Once inside they made fresh soup, sipped limply from their mugs, cursed the respective days on which they had been born, and fell asleep on scattered hay.

Melker grew colder in his writing bunker. Resting his pen, he rubbed his hands. "That's enough." He sniffed the air and collected what he had written. He tied the new pages into the manuscript and locked them in his trunk. "For now," he added as he creaked upwards.

Spying the chickens through a crack in the wall, he spotted who he needed to kill. He decided to postpone the event and walked outside through the fallen snow, uneven earth, and patches of browned grass to his favourite stream. He sat on the bank to think. Clearing the snow, he touched the small rocks. He threw a rock in the stream where it plunked. "What a contemptible life. But how could it be any other way?" He then composed a verse and recited,

> Stands a poet on the brink
> Sans sidekick he cannot think
> Depths he judges shallow become
> A girl, a boy, index a thumb
> For, in misconceptions there are truths
> Cheese to milk, calcium, and tooth
> Yet heaviness is not impossible
> Food is repetitive, love improbable.

Next moment he remembered something that he thought he had forgotten. He recalled the words from memory and rephrased them into a Melker-stamped series of sentences:

"The slingshot theory suggests that any remark which is true corresponds to the same fact...the fact of life...but most people find this impossible which makes the correspondence theory dissipate like steam." He laughed. "But everything certainly corresponds to one thing. Every stream of living originates from the same mouth of the river. That's why salmon swim upstream to lay their eggs: they return physically and mentally from whence they came." The stream ran on as snow hit the ground almost silently. "What we call eerie silences are merely peaceful. We are not used to peace," said Melker as he composed even more verse in his head,

> On this lonely day, a thousand more
> Defining warming, breathing, chide, and bore
> It's hate which makes the chickens grow
> The thicker the clouds, the less I know
> Disguising cheer is bleak disgust
> Family tools covered in rust
> Falling, I cannot ignore
> Eyes within me scan the shore

Surrounding the Chicken Boy was now a mountain range of typed documents. Obscuring his body from the Metaphysical Circus, the piles of paper shifted and flopped down.

The Astrologer and the Strongman had been building props, but noticing the white border of the typed documents, took a break, and flipped a coin to see who would investigate.

The Astrologer went over to the Chicken Boy, who barely acknowledged her. "Hello little one," she said with a grimace, "what's all this you've made?"

What had he written? What did this mean?

He stared numbly at the typewriter, the current page trapped in the roll. The Astrologer pulled the sheet out of the typewriter, scanned the sheet, and turned white.

"*Act Three. Scene One. A Street. Enter Cassio and Musicians,*" read the Astrologer. "*Cassio.* Masters, play here. I will content your pains—You two! Come here! Quickly!"

Watching this with anguish, the Maestro rushed over and was followed by the Strongman who creaked over from the stage and prepared himself for a duel of rhetoric.

"What are you doing to my darling star?" asked the Maestro with bated breath.

"Leave her alone," interrupted the Strongman. "She's the only one who's been paying attention to him." He looked at the piles of documents and chuckled. "As far as the mountain range is concerned don't ask me for sources."

Despite the Maestro being taller than the Astrologer, he stared up at her and sneered. "I'm sure that you have done something. Hallucinogenic drugs?" he suggested violently. "Why else would he be staring ahead like a dolt?"

"Look at this! Here's evidence of my innocence!" said the Astrologer as she forced a sheet of paper into the Maestro's sweaty palms.

Barely looking at the sheet of paper the Maestro flapped it when he spoke. "Why do you always waste my time? I don't want you to copy out your lines. I want you to learn them."

"For God's sakes—*the Chicken Boy wrote it*," replied the Astrologer.

"What do you mean the Chicken Boy wrote *Othello?*" chuckled the Maestro cynically. "The stink of alcohol has dissipated—but your brain is still fogged."

"He typed the page you're holding."

Looking between her and the sheet of paper, he exploded. "What a pack of nonsense! You blame my darling star because you lack his unique talents!"

Raising his eyebrows, the Strongman shifted his huge feet awkwardly.

"You are a jealous clairvoyant who has no skill in her craft. That goes for the both of you. You and the *Weakman* get back to work before I fetch my bullwhip."

Shaking his head in frustration the Strongman took a deep breath, picked up a small pack of papers, and shoved them into the Maestro's inflated chest. "I want you to listen to *her*," threatened the Strongman. "Do you notice something when you look at these pages? What's clear when you open your eyes is that he's been refining these words for hours and hours. The writing is barely legible if we examine this sheet. But here! The words take shape when we examine this sheet." He jabbed an index finger into his chest. "Don't accuse her of wasting your time. She's been with me the whole time busting her arse—"

"Maybe…" whispered the Maestro. "Impossible! He's beautiful because he's stupid! He's simple and easy to master. I've mastered him over the years. I'm an employer, not a lover. I don't even…I don't know what I'm saying."

Suddenly, the Chicken Boy lifted his beaked face: "Othello is alone. Soldiers and senators ruin the frame. Betrayal sullies personal bones and deshackles sentiments wise and tame. The abortion breaks the state and crafts self-apology and hate..."

"That's not what I made of the play—but there you go," said the Strongman practically.

The Maestro was beside himself with anguish. "Hallucinogenic drugs! You have ruined everything with your narcotics! I predict that without our star attraction, we're going to wither!" Then staring angrily at the typewriter, the Maestro kicked the machine, held his foot, and regained his posture. "Who placed him before this mechanical monstrosity?"

"But it was just there. He went to it willingly," explained the Astrologer.

"Don't talk to me about will. He hasn't sufficient brain power for will. He's simple and easy to master. He wouldn't know determination if it hatched an egg on his head!"

Without warning a tenor voice manifested itself. "You should re-consider the word or attempt to empathize with something you misconstrue as being of less value than yourself..." The voice was stern. The voice was tough. The voice came from the Chicken Boy.

Insulted the Maestro looked down his nose. "The creation turns upon his master. You must have feigned retardation from the very beginning," he derided. "You betrayed me. You betrayed the Metaphysical Circus. Worst of all you betrayed yourself. I fear I may kill myself."

"You're too *cynical* to self-murder," replied the Chicken Boy.

"What did you say to me?" hissed the Maestro.

Standing up the Chicken Boy brushed invisible powder from his shoulders. He stared down his former master, scratched his feet against the concrete, and scoffed unpleasantly.

Arriving on the scene, Drast and Pommel huffed bureaucratically. "What is this commotion?" asked Drast as he lowered the habit's perimeter onto the tanned tops of his feet. "Angeloff can't learn his lines with all this turmoil going on in the background—"

In a flurry of movement, the Chicken Boy threw Drast to the ground and stood triumphantly over the quivering body. "Do not lecture me on recitation," announced the Chicken Boy as Drast cowered beneath him. "I doubt that you comprehend the nature of these typewriters. You are content to water the garden of ignorance with your reckless stupidity." Holding his hands behind his back, the Chicken Boy paced in circles. "I am free to speak. I am afraid. I am terrified." He paused. "What are these words...that plague my mind? I dwell in this pit of language and knowledge. Do you know my pain?" he asked with genuine sorrow.

"Shut up, you dork," replied the Maestro.

"The truth is that you surprise no one. That's why you hate yourself. You punish the people who work for you and have no other pleasures," diagnosed the Chicken Boy as he waved a feathery hand. "But the words you speak are nothing so nasty as my own. Where is that silence that I once cherished? What happened to those dim pastures? Where a rock was a rock? Where a fool was a fool? The wind used to lick my skin and make no thinking. I shall never lease my life to misery as *you* do with such alacrity. Let that be my warning," he told the Maestro. "You treated me like an animal... only worse...I banish myself on pain of death."

"You shall have it," promised the Maestro as his star attraction strutted away, through the doorway and down the stairs. "You will pay tenfold for ruining my circus. That's what you get for teaching things how to read. Why would any creature consent to that education?"

"Don't look at *me*," replied the Astrologer. "I couldn't teach him how to boil an egg. I'm sick to death of doing the cooking all of the damn time," she added. "I work day in and day out for your stupid show."

Deflated the Maestro turned to the larger employee. "What about you? I bet you're as strong as soup when confronted with the facts."

"I can barely read myself. I overhear everything I know. A good noggin for memory but little else," confessed the Strongman.

The Maestro scoffed.

"Can we agree that the Chicken Boy didn't read *Othello*?" suggested the Astrologer. "But he seemed to write it from memory."

"That's more impossible than his learning how to type," blustered the Maestro through yet another important point. "May I remind you that we plan to perform the damn play?"

"But he didn't know that. He wasn't aware of that. Except the typewriter…brought the words out of him as though he found the mouth of the river…"

Marielle Agapov laid Plum Lukum onto the mattress of hay and looked around the room for consolation. "The Kanchil deity—the mousedeer," babbled Lukum as she subconsciously wriggled into a more comfortable position on her back. "It pretends to have powers it does not have. By doing this it frightens away predators who would otherwise eat it."

Agapov fetched an unsanitary quilt, flopped it over Lukum, and pulled it up to her chin.

"I wish I could have done that. If on the other hand, I possessed imaginary powers…I would have told the Bluebloods that I could chop oceans with my hands. I would have told them that my white hair burned the night sky when given half a chance. It was not so white in those days. I had colour. I would have told them that should anyone touch my hair they would die instantly," said Lukum as she watched the earthy ceiling click with condensation. "What would they have done when they realized I was lying? I would have ended up here—because all roads lead to the wasteland. All roads lead to this hovel, this existence. It would seem that I have no control over my fate…only I want to pretend that I do…because in doing so I increase my misery tenfold…"

She stopped talking. Scanning the room for people she found none. She realized that Agapov too had disappeared.

"Gone," decided Lukum. "Vaporized like dust in the hurricane. The farmers shall not have her." She frowned and bared her teeth. "They will all be dead soon."

Unbeknownst to Plum Lukum, the erstwhile guest had wandered across the wasteland. The wind was high, the snow was heavy and fell in great clumps onto Agapov's shivering shoulders. Plodding ahead, she forced one foot in front of the other as her mind focused on locomotion. Her feet froze when she stopped and her eyes zoomed in on the mud beneath the snow. Her mouth was dry. She collapsed and her body tumbled down an incline leading to a loud stream. She watched the snow falling as she lay there on her back. Falling asleep, she finally thanked God.

Fibber staggered over to the crushed remains of Marshall Volkov. He was moved as the chaos unfolded—butchers, bakers, and publicans fought over typewriters. They paid no mind to the man who up until his death had represented workers in industrial disputes cleverly controlled by the Blueblood Government.

"Volkov is mangled," muttered Fibber. Novikoff stood awkwardly behind him. "What has happened to this man improves upon the cruelty administered in the Legend of Tsar Saltan," continued Fibber as he caressed his painful knees.

Suddenly, Marielle Agapov's ex-children appeared from out of the crowd. The boy still wore nothing else but the raincoat as he slapped his naked feet through the wet rubble. The girl was wearing the same potato sack with holes cut out for arms; her blonde hair was dirtier than before. "Take the typewriters to your tents and keep them safe," ordered the boy. "They belong to us because the people outside betrayed their country. They don't have our luck!"

Taking his hand, the girl nodded seriously. "The weirdo told us about the writer in the wasteland," she explained. "But he's no better than the Bluebloods. We have to write!"

"You little monsters," alleged Fibber as more people fought over the typewriters. "I'm going to grill you in our beloved furnace."

"Our words will beat your words," screamed the girl as Fibber chased them both away. A butcher's ankle stopped him in his tracks and he touched the floor and caught his breath.

"Maybe Volkov was right about Lenin and people and their compulsions. I may be compelled to misery like the very best nineteenth-century characters. Why don't we open a shop and sell misery by the bloody pound?" Then Fibber saw Volkov's hand in the rubble. "My emotions proved him wrong."

One of the swirling culinary figures punched Fibber. Falling to one side, Fibber touched his lip and wiped the blood on the ground. "Malark just *had* to split them from their caretaker…"

Novikoff patted his back. "We're all monsters in here. We're condemned to sit out the invasion—"

He slapped her hand away. "What invasion?"

"Is this true?"

"What I think I retain. What I retain is phenomenal for my eyes. In other words: access denied," hissed Fibber as he stood up and leaned upon a chain. "I became a writer because I wanted to purge my sensations. But what's happened is that nowhere is a place and I inhabit it flawlessly. I have things that need doing or finding out." He paused and coughed. "Angeloff."

"Pistachio trees. They grow towards the sun," advised Novikoff.

"Then I go up. I'll go that way." He dragged the carcass of Marshall Volkov to the wall where there was a chute labeled "furnace". Opening the hatch, Fibber carefully pushed Volkov's body into it and the silence that followed the cadaver's crossing was moving.

Fibber identified the staircase to the third floor and resolved to make the journey.

On the verge of killing the chicken, Melker relented and returned to his favourite stream. Once there, he found a lump covered in snow which he soon realized was a person. Brushing away the white dust he found a woman wearing an emerald waistcoat and an ankle-length dress. Her knee-length metal boots were chafing against her skin and her frizzy red hair seemed to have lost its colour. "Are you alright?" the writer asked the apparent corpse. "My poetry couldn't have done this to you—as if suddenly my poetry strikes you down as you're walking along."

The corpse opened her eyes. "Where am I?" moaned Agapov.

"Where you are," replied Melker as he picked her up. "I will take you home. You must have been walking for hours."

He put his arm around her and walked her over snowy earth. They went for a while in silence and Melker became anxious.

Agapov kept opening and shutting her mouth. "Do you...have anything to eat?"

"Not on me; just at home," replied Melker. "Don't fall asleep. You must not do that. You may have to help me murder a chicken."

Agapov said nothing.

"I know it sounds brutal. But farm life is like that."

"You're out of practice," whispered Agapov.

"You can't be out of practice when you have never done something." He spied the sky. "It's beginning to get dark—we need to hurry."

"I've had...nothing but grass soup...for two days..."

"You're not a polymath by any chance?"

A well-sized chunk of silence trickled through cascading snowflakes. "No," she said.

"I was wondering if I could talk to you about something: a certain subject I've been considering for some time. I have no intention of lording my brain over you—I just want to jabber away," explained Melker in that tone often used by groundsmen.

"Go ahead," replied Agapov. She trudged her feet through the snow and watched the earth.

"Excellent, excellent. There is something in logic called the quality of propositions. These are qualities a proposition can have. They can either be positive or negative. But I've been thinking we are limiting ourselves if we reduce logic to a dichotomy of qualities," began Melker. "What I mean by this statement is that, surely, propositions must have other qualities apart from being either positive or negative. We could use these other qualities in hypotheses, calculations, and ideas—ones that go beyond logic. It's quite fascinating!" he exclaimed. What I find is that my brain will go off on a tangent—but maybe it only does that when I'm thinking about logic. It's for this reason, perhaps, that logic has to be dichotomized and reductionist. Imagine for a moment a logic that is expansive and multifaceted. There is such a thing as fuzzy logic, for example, where propositions show a degree of truth and nothing more; this would be perfect were it not for those same degrees arising from within the logical complex. It only seems to pretend to be open-minded. That's my opinion. What do you think?"

The woman's body had taken over from her mind. It piloted her carefully over the uneven ground and allowed the arms to swing pendulously as the mind went on holiday.

Tightening his grip, he thought about fuzzy logic and where it had all gone wrong. "We have a long way to go," muttered Melker. The stars above them led the way back to the farm where a pre-determined chicken contemplated what it would do to keep warm that night.

The wealthiest families made the third floor their home. They built makeshift houses and embraced the typewriter craze with great religion. But Timofey Popov and Pavel Grinko were two young men who thought everything was boring, estranging themselves from their wealthy families as well as the poverty below them. The boys drank heavily and paraded themselves through crumbling excess and mumbling writers. "I'm going to fight someone," promised Pavel as they avoided more people using typewriters. His skin was deathly pale and he was incredibly skinny. He looked over at his friend who drained another vodka miniature. "Give me someone to fight," muttered Pavel. "You don't know a damn thing about fighting but if you find me a bastard then I will show you. I would give them a quick right in the jawbone… a knee in the groin…that should knock the bastard silly. If you find me someone, I will make them fall like lemmings… because behind the bastard will be one hundred more bastards. Come on, Timofey, stand up."

"Can't you see how sozzled I am?" asked Timofey. His brown hair teased the backs of his large ears and the way he stood was as though he had placed a large bet on something dead. "We have been sozzled for hours. What are you talking about?"

"If you can't find me a bastard to fight then I will fight you," threatened Pavel.

"We're supposed to be friends." He itched his ears. "Why should I want to fight you?"

"I wish the Tectum had a body. I'd fight him to the death—the big-headed bastard."

"You don't have to prove anything. Just have a good time," sighed Timofey.

"There's no good time in life. That's the wrong fashion with which to look at the universe. You're a mess because your life has bad times: a fight with me is sure to be one of them."

"It would be a good time for you?"

"It goes deeper than that." Draining a bottle of beer, Pavel smashed it on the ground. "I'm a convoluted individual." Aiming bloodshot eyes, he saw Fibber appear from the staircase.

"Who's that?" asked Timofey as he swallowed a teaspoon of sick.

"I'll knock the pistachio dust off him," hissed Pavel.

Fibber grabbed the nearest chain. He glared at them. "What?"

"Nothing," replied Pavel quickly.

"Listen you two—" He was out of breath as he clinked towards them. "I need to know if you've seen a man called *Angeloff*—He has two accomplices. Have you seen them?"

"Can you find the midget who stole our beer?" asked Pavel rudely. "He went upstairs but there are crazy people up there."

"That sounds about right. We're putting on *Othello*. By the way that midget you mentioned is a dwarf."

Timofey gasped. "Are you the Overseer? The real one? I've read your poetry!"

"We don't talk about the poetry," warned Fibber as he tapped his nose and squinted with one eye.

"*With violent hog and rabbit, my dreamscapes geese inhabit—*"

"Shut up," interrupted Fibber. "Have you seen anyone suspicious, then?"

"No," replied Pavel as he gurned. "I would've beat them with my sickening fists."

"Mmm."

"We have a problem, Overseer," explained Timofey. "Pavel won't shut up about being the best fighter in the camp. Could you prove him wrong by throwing him over your shoulder? I don't want you to kill him. I just want him to learn his lesson. But if it's about money, I can vouch for my family's wealth—"

"But I'm the wealthier," instructed Pavel. "I'm happy to pay you—but be warned."

"How does that sound?" Timofey tugged Fibber's sleeve.

Fibber nodded inwardly. It would be a longer day than he had expected. "Fifty drachmas for the fight. Twenty drachmas for medical bills," came his offer.

Pavel smiled. "I like your style, you bastard—" They exchanged drachmas in a flurry of overlapping hands. Timofey watched the money passing hands with the wild grin of hubris.

Satisfied after counting the drachmas, Fibber wrapped them together using a rubber band and then hid them on his person. "Are we going to fight here?"

"I can only presume you prefer padded flooring. That way when I throw your skull down you will be protected," judged Pavel. "But I prefer to fight here, you bastard."

"Very well." He removed the bubbly green coat and his white undershirt.

"I don't care about your protective pistachio layer."

"You're dead, Pavel," said Timofey in half-serious horror.

"You begin to get scared!" laughed Pavel behind sickly raised fists. "You move well for a poet...I've heard crazy things about you…I'm not surprised that you find yourself patrolling neurones." He threw a punch that kissed the air. "How do you like that metaphor? I have two more—"

Fibber smacked the boy down with two bursts. He then grabbed his belt and slammed him head-first into a pile of potatoes.

A brief silence followed. As Pavel regained consciousness, he smelled his trousers and felt the invisible reputation as the greatest fighter in the camp melt limply into the ether.

"Destroyed!" declared Timofey.

Forcing on his white undershirt and bubbly green jacket, Fibber viewed his opponent. "Are you okay?" Pavel crawled out of the potatoes. He cried as he held a bloody nose. "Okay," comforted Fibber, "it's alright…"

"I can't do anything right!" whimpered Pavel.

Like a damsel in distress, Fibber picked him up. "It's alright," repeated Fibber.

Timofey dusted his hands and whistled. "Is he okay?"

"I just punched him in the fucking face. Is there a doctor here?"

Timofey pointed towards an elaborate tent. "That tent," squalled Pavel, "over there."

"Thanks for the drachmas but I have nothing to spend it on," said Fibber as he clomped towards the tent and heard Timofey crack open his last vodka miniature. "Don't worry, Pavel. You are going to live."

"I'm such a loser," mewled Pavel.

"We all feel that way. It's okay."

He carried the boy through typing alleys and strolled inside the tent where an orange candlelight was soothing. His boots dirtied the Persian carpets that lined the floors and marked the walls. On the far side of the tent, a medical curtain wiggled. Behind it, someone washed their hands. "Is there a doctor in the house?" asked Fibber.

Dr. Nikolai Grinko came into view as he flicked his large hands free of water. His curled moustache was bushy and bright black. He was wearing a red waistcoat over a mint-green shirt, black corduroy trousers, and pointy boots whose tips shone like far-away planets. "I thought I'd get away from my discipline for a time," he rasped with the remnants of authority. "But there are festering sores that need cauterizing in the head." He beckoned them closer and squinted. "My son has had another fight. Fantastic. Put him down there."

Fibber rested Pavel on a patch of uneven linen and backed away as the paterfamilias approached ruefully with his stethoscope. "You have survived again. You will live to fight another day," declared Grinko as he faffed about with his waistcoat. "Here's a lollipop for you. Brush your teeth afterwards." As he stared at the lollipop, Pavel sobbed and lowered his head.

Noticing the sweaty man standing in his surgery, Doctor Grinko twirled his moustache. "What on earth is Dante Fibber doing here? You should be downstairs with the poor folk."

Pavel banged the lollipop against his back. "Papa! Please talk to me!"

"Hush, my son. Your father has an important guest."

"But I'm your son! Please, can't we talk?" He quieted down when Fibber smiled at him. He touched his pink tongue against the lollipop and then sniffled gently for a few moments.

"Dostoyevsky writes *The Double* after *Poor Folk*," Fibber said to Doctor Grinko. "The book didn't make any money because no one could figure out what he was talking about. His epilepsy got much worse during this time because he was stressed. But I think his double took over and wrote *Crime and Punishment, Notes from Underground,* and *Brothers Karamazov.* This means that the original Dostoyevsky wrote nothing apart from those two early novels. This is good news for you, Pavel, because you are the original, and you are going to live."

"There's no other bastard like me," said Pavel with some pride.

"That's right; you're the original and you are going to live!"

"Absolutely remarkable," said Doctor Grinko as he almost snapped his moustache off. "Pavel, why don't you join your friends outside?"

"They're not friends," replied Pavel quietly. "I'm their bastard."

"Go in the back and get some sleep. Then prepare yourself to be cheered. We are going to have prawn risotto tonight," rasped Doctor Grinko as he nodded with encouragement.

"Okay…" Shuffling behind the curtain Pavel sucked modestly on his lollipop.

Then Doctor Grinko smiled at Fibber and gestured amiably. "Tea?"

"Please," agreed Fibber. "What's your name?"

"Nikolai Grinko—" He roamed behind the curtain where he disappeared. "Up until a week ago, I ran a clinic. I was arrested when I campaigned for a national health-care. This played havoc with Pavel." There was a glugging sound and then some clanking. "I have found that what men and women have in common, they make up for with their mutual lack of self-esteem. Pavel is my case study as well as my son…" He returned carrying two teacups as well as a small gas cooker. He lighted the cooker using a long match and then placed the kettle on top. "I'm not a monster," muttered Doctor Grinko as he listened for whistling. "It's the only way we can build a functioning society."

"Healthcare?"

"Ours on the other hand can only function at the high-est levels. But as for the lower levels—" He looked at Fibber, smiled, and then nodded leftward. "I make strong tea."

"I'm the Overseer here." Fibber spoke as though he were showing Doctor Grinko how a combustion engine worked.

"You must have done something naughty."

"There was a magazine launch in someone's house. I went to the party afterwards. But the police had an ear somewhere."

"Sufficed to say that corroborates everything that I have heard." He shrugged. "Thelonious Fibber pales in compari-son to his nephew."

Fibber smiled.

"In my experience, Fascists are frightened of words. Per-haps this goes back to the power-hungry fearing the Greek republic," recalled Doctor Grinko as the kettle climaxed and sighed. "But representation has its own problems. On occasion, I can see no difference between the tyrants of old and our current representatives." He stopped talking as he made the tea. "You won't find *me* touching those typewriters," he said with pride.

Given his geographical position, Captain Gurkin changed his mind. There arose a development that needed to be executed immediately and prompted Private Rakovsky to change course. It was early evening and the snow had ceased altogether. The raid tank ruined the earth as it turned round. In about half an hour, the violent vehicle reached the sandy clearing where it sped inexorably into Plum Lukum's hovel. Then it reversed leaving a gaping hole where the thatched door had once stood. Rakovsky cut the engines as Captain Gurkin emerged from the hatch.

The dissident stumbled from the ruins of her erstwhile habitation. "You will put an end to me! I am finally going to die!" she shouted with glee as her rickety legs delivered her.

Gurkin squeaked through the snow with a submachine gun.

"Shoot me! Shoot me!" demanded Lukum.

When he fired a train-track of geysers cut through the snow towards Plum Lukum. A library of small books unzipped themselves on her chest and she fell backwards onto the snow.

Gurkin lowered the smoking barrel. He addressed Rakovsky who had emerged from the hatch. "The other one must be inside," instructed Gurkin as he pointed with ambivalence.

Rakovsky lowered himself into the raid tank where he grabbed a nearby joystick. He flicked a switch and pulled the creaky trigger. Outside an arc of flame shot from the raid tank and reduced what remained of the hovel to an inferno. Gurkin returned inside the raid tank and shut the hatch. The vicious engines chugged back to life. The machine marred the wasteland as it returned to the city.

Melker was staring at the chickens. He was getting cold and time was running out. He grabbed the fowl and prayed for the neck to snap when he twisted it. Like the blackest night, success dawned upon him. He ignored his tears and scraped his boots before entering the house...

Inside the house, Marielle Agapov was dishevelled and sitting at the kitchen table sipping broth. Marina was opposite her with folded arms and a diamond-cut gaze. Olga was setting the table when Melker appeared in the doorway, the deceased chicken dangling from his right hand which quivered with adrenaline and intellectual regret.

"I tried to make it quick but it felt like murder," said Melker.

"What do you know about murder outside of your books?" said Marina. "Hand it over."

He passed the chicken to Marina who plucked it at the table.

"Put a cloth down," warned Olga.

"It's not like you to waste cloth. Melker shouldn't bring strange women home." Marina glanced up from the dead chicken. "Where are you from?"

Agapov swallowed. "The city."

"We used to be from the city. We adopted Melker when I worked in the parliamentary buildings—" She offered a glance to Olga that stank of geometric precision. "Did you know that egg whites and salts can be used to tenderize chicken? The chemistry keeps my cooking fresh." The wind howled outside. "You have the air of someone who tenderized another."

"But she's our guest," hissed Olga.

Marina sniggered. "Do you think we came here by accident? The wasteland has never seen accidents and it never shall. You must have killed someone," she told Agapov.

"My husband," she replied. "My stupid, ignorant husband."

Plucking happily from the chicken's rump, Marina was wholly unconcerned. "If you try that in here, you're going to end up like this chicken."

She handed the plucked chicken to Olga, produced a tin and rolling papers, and rolled a large cigarette. "I'm going to have a smoke."

Melker made to stand but Marina whistled and he sat down. She licked the edges of the paper and poked the end between her lips. She struck a match on the table and took a long suck. "I can't believe that you broke out of the Tectum." She paused for effect. "That thing is impregnable."

"I wasn't allowed…to go inside."

"That person will hang. It was a strange time when they were building." All they could hear was Olga chopping the chicken into chunks of meat when she stopped talking. "It

took them a decade to build the Tectum. The whole operation was done in secret and using migrant workers. They
brought them in from the seven empires. We were ordered to
never speak to them and they worked all year round—dying
like flies. When everything was finished, they gathered the
workers and shot them. There was a mass grave which was
buried and forgotten." She took a long drag on her cigarette.
"I have heard that they are trying to find God…"

In her damp office, Minister Jozlov collected sensitive
papers and shoved them into a briefcase. The remaining
papers, which were less sensitive, were shoved into a bin,
doused in rice wine, and set alight. The paper twisted into
grey shapes irradiated by wriggling orange lines of flame.
Inspecting the unrecognizable remains, Minister Jozlov bat-
ted out the fire and prowled towards the door. Sweaty and
nervous, she turned the knob and moved to enter the corridor. But Malark was on the other side.

"It will be a cold day in hell when your type mixes
with the riffraff out here," he said politely. "Are you going
somewhere?"

A drip of condensation tapped her forehead. "I would
have stayed here and faced Desdemona's fate if my mother
had employed a maid called Barbary. But seeing as she didn't,
I wouldn't waste my time standing there when you have a
play to produce."

"Intuition denotes how something is known. What you
think about me and what I get up to are two different things."

"I'm much obliged for your ambiguity—I must leave now."

"A millipede couldn't get in—let alone a Belgian army," replied Malark as he put a finger on one nostril and blew out of the other. "I've dedicated some thought to whether we can develop the Tectum. For example, if we spread out the Tectum would it stretch or flatten."

She smiled as she breathed heavily through wide nostrils. "I have important business that I can't put off any longer."

He kicked the door and stepped inside. "Geometry won't save you," said Malark as he locked the door behind him, turned round, and winced. "Where are you going?"

Jozlov shuddered. "I can pay you if that's what you want. There are drachmas and other things…"

"I wish to paint you in the style of a Thabet: the spirit of a woman who died in childbirth." He looked at his feet and grew angry. "Those whores down the hallway refused to model for me. In any case, they know too much about childbirth."

"You're in grave danger," warned Jozlov. "They told me to stay in an official capacity. But they can't fool me." Then walking in circles, she seemed to be confirming her suspicions.

"It does not take a genius to work out that people die when there is architecture involved. Once upon a time, when we were building this place, I was the Overseer. I've seen the designs. They show an exit route—but I know for a fact that it was never built."

"Then why is it shown?" asked Malark with a strange expression.

"I refuse to subscribe to the same fate as yours—"

"Take off your clothes."

"I beg your pardon?"

"I'm going to sketch you so that I can paint you later," explained Malark.

The minister and the deputy overseer looked at one another. But they both conceived the universe as being a place where time was perpetually running out and a scarce resource.

"No!" denied Jozlov.

"I can't deny what I am," said Malark. "I have exorcized my excess energy with prostitutes and am now ready to work. I used to do this every week. This time it took me a matter of days. Lucian Freud used to wear blinkers in hospitals because he didn't want to see the nurses. But now the blinkers are off, minister—What do you call a racist nineteenth-century artist?"

"I don't care and I refuse to get naked!"

"An oppresionist," replied Malark as he produced a pad and pencil from his trousers. "I'll help you find a way out if you model for me. But if you refuse me, I'll have to go downstairs and find a callow peasant for a few drachmas."

Jozlov lowered her briefcase. "Do you promise?"

"I am your lifeline," vouched Malark. "If you are crazy enough to break out, then I am crazy enough to join you. But without the work, we might as well not discuss these things."

Jozlov removed her robes and then her undergarments. She stood naked for the deputy overseer who was a consummate professional.

"On the chair, please. Bring it round here for me," instructed Malark as the high-backed chair was dragged into view. "Legs crossed. Put your left hand on the arm. Let the right arm droop by your side. That's perfect. I won't be long." He silenced himself and sketched.

Jozlov peered at the artist. "I thought we might go through the furnace—"

"We don't want to be here all night," explained Malark. "We'll be finished in twenty minutes if neither of us speaks." He sketched again and broke his rule. "We can make our way through the furnace when the night shift comes into effect. As a matter of fact, all painters are hypocrites…"

Unbeknownst to Jozlov and Malark hundreds of people were using typewriters throughout the Tectum. Their fingers blistered as they rolled inexorable sheets of paper onto the drums. Perhaps the writing would save them from something. But if so, what?

Her nicotine-stained fingers rolled another large cigarette. Lifting the cigarette to her lips, Marina bit down, sucked brownish smoke into her lungs, and puffed it into the kitchen. "There is something about those typewriters in the Tectum: it draws people towards them and makes them use them. They write, words, sentences, paragraphs, and pages of nonsensical stuff. We know they are not writing *Hamlet*, for example, but in that case, what are they writing?" The wind outside was deafening as she went on. "We know that plays don't happen like that. They take time. But those Bluebloods want to prove this wrong—because if they do, they'll be proving that a higher power exists."

She nodded at Melker who went around clearing the table after supper. He carried plates to the sink where he covered them in water and started scrubbing them.

"The Bluebloods have sabotaged themselves," argued Marina as she puffed pensively.

"They have not given those people ample time to prove this; there is one recourse to failure." Through the window she watched splotch-upon-splotch of snow piling up outside. "What that storm kicks up will be nothing compared to what will happen when those lab mice put away their typewriters." She coughed. "We'll dig ourselves out tomorrow morning."

"How long…have they got?" Agapov paled.

"Half the time that God had," replied Marina as Melker made for his jacket. "You can't go outside—you'll freeze to death."

"Someone needs to document this."

Throwing her cigarette away Marina bolted upright. "No. I forbid you. We'll be hanged. Nor does your friend put us in a good position—"

"Every year liberties are removed from the body of the state. Bills that contradict other bills. Bills that damn and destroy. The only thing that will be left is our literature—"

"Cheap propaganda," shouted Marina.

"My work recalls a time when there was expression. It's no secret that the state pays me to write my novels. But those same novels contain the pumpkin seeds of revolution! I have never endorsed the state. But I never exchanged my heart for my brain."

"I have a cease-and-desist chain hanging around my neck," hissed Marina. "You act as though you are exempt from all of this."

"You won't stop me," said Melker as he pulled on his jacket. "Not this time—"

"We have to work together. We can't do that if you freeze to death."

"I don't want to survive—I want to live!"

Agapov shot up with a knife in her hand, pressed the blade against Marina's throat, and looked around the kitchen for anyone who wished to contest her violent grasp of the situation. Marina gasped as she raised her hands in appeasement.

"Don't hurt her!" screamed Melker. Olga stood by him. "What are you doing?"

"Relax," muttered Marina as the unsharpened blade grated against her wrinkled skin. "The beast will issue her demands," she coughed. "I know her type. She's predictable."

"Wise old bird," agreed Agapov.

"I don't have much meat on me—and you're hurting my arm."

"The writer...get away from the door," instructed Agapov. "You own a rover and keep it next to the shed."

"It's knackered," promised Melker.

"You can fix it." Her eyes betrayed elastic nerves pulled to the snapping point. "You're going to drive me to the city. When you've done that, you'll come back here. No diversions."

"They'll shoot you on sight," said Olga. She knew what the City Council was like.

Using her feet like levers Agapov inched Marina in the direction of the doorway. "Richard Strauss wrote an opera called *A Hero's Life* that was meant to be a sequel to *Don Quixote*. But everyone thought it was about how Strauss fought the critics and tried to be famous. What proves this is how he lifted from earlier works while he was writing the opera. But I've no intention of listening to a pair of patriarchal lesbians—"

The flesh loosened on the right side of her face. Fighting against her own body, Agapov accidentally let go of Marina who joined her family on the other side of the kitchen. "She's an epileptic," declared Marina as the seizure broke Agapov and she collapsed onto the floorboards.

"On the contrary," replied Olga, "she can't eat white flour. That's why I put some in the marengo."

Focusing slowly on her wife, Marina couldn't believe her ears. "How did you know?"

"A starving woman didn't want bread with her broth." Her eyes betrayed nothing. "Get me the gun, Melker."

Melker didn't move. Did he hear that right?

"Don't just stand there." Olga looked at him. "Get me the gun, Melker."

Melker snuck out of the room as Agapov writhed on the floorboards. He returned with a rifle and a box of ammo and gave them to his mother. "You're going to shoot her?" burbled Marina as her wife duly charged the rifle with ammo and released the safety latch.

"They shan't know." She aimed the rifle. "They'll never know what happened."

"But...what can be done with the body?"

"The hogs have had nothing but slops for three months."

Sensing the danger Agapov tensed her body. "*Help me...*"

"Help is coming," replied Olga as she aimed the rifle, fired, and then supplied the first explosive fissure with another apple-sized cavern.

"Clean up this mess," ordered Olga as she re-positioned the safety latch and rested the rifle on the table. "She can rest in the storeroom. The hogs can have her in the morning." Turning to Melker, who was sweating and watching in horror, she snapped her fingers. "You're not going to write about this. You just keep writing that propaganda; do you understand?"

"Yes, mama," came the reply.

"You became a man today. You can finish those dishes."

Melker returned to the sink where he scrubbed cutlery, a dazed expression on his face. In the meantime, Olga turned her attention to Marina who was standing motionless and fatigued.

"Oh—get on with it, you stupid shrew!" shouted Olga who then watched her remove the body.

The interior of the covered wagon was illuminated by candlelight. Honza broke bread with the Maestro, the Bearded Lady, the Strongman, and the Astrologer. The candlelight shrunk their faces and their fingers excavated shadows as they accused bodies. Honza took the Chicken Boy's bunk and went through his script for *Othello* trying to learn his extremely long lines.

Picking crumbs out of his sizeable beard, the Bearded Lady bred a smirk. "I've got a poem brewing in my stomach," he said disdainfully. "It's about our director..."

"I'm praying," grumbled the Maestro as he mourned the Chicken Boy's departure.

Softening the bread with her saliva, the Astrologer patted him on the back. "The Chicken Boy belongs with those bankers and intellectuals. You'll find another star attraction." She chewed quietly. "I'm resentful it won't be me. But you can't have everything."

Bumping his head on the ceiling, the Strongman winced. "The suspense is killing me."

In his bunk, Honza threw down his script. "I've got people telling me all day to learn my goddamn lines and you're just sitting there eating bread," moaned Honza. "It's a damn shame."

"That bastard Grinko can work out your anal fistula for free," said the Astrologer.

"You need to worry about your weight."

"And you need to worry about your height."

"I love your hair," hissed Honza. "How'd you get it to come out of your nostrils?"

"One of the family." She squinted. "The Manson Family."

"If you're gonna be two-faced, make sure one of them is pretty."

"I know you are but what am I?"

"Fuck this." Turning onto his side Honza went to sleep. The Astrologer smiled wryly at the Bearded Lady who rubbed his hands together. He cleared his mind and recited,

Overseer, what do you require?
Pension, poppies on the grave at midnight
Overseer, whom do you inspire?
Punter, pauper, strongman, an errant knight?
Care not for you, these people do and sing
Insults over hypocrisies, they fling
Listeners, I have irritated through
Though, if I'm the sinner, then who be you?

Honza had only pretended to fall asleep. "Next time you look in the mirror," he said without turning around, "why don't you say hello to the world's worst poet?"

Elsewhere, in the vast expanse of the fourth floor, Drast and Pommel were sitting around the proverbial campfire where they took turns reading Iago's lines to Angeloff.

"*As I am an honest man, I thought you had received some bodily wound,*" Drast read from the book after which he cast it down. "I've had enough. I can't take it anymore." Poking the fire with crusts of bread he then pinched the bridge of his nose and looked at Angeloff. His eyes were grey and dead and the curl of black hair that descended over his forehead looked sad. Drast stared at that permanent straight line of observed silence that was Angeloff's mouth. Then he returned his eyes to Angeloff's dull grey peepers. "The man's eyes give me no wisdom," said Drast. "Do you think I'll have to make placards so that he can read his lines?"

"You have no faith," replied Pommel. "Many acolytes departed the order when Angeloff took his vow of silence."

"You said he had a cold! A vow of silence! What do you think you're doing giving him a role in the play? There are more lines here than a fucking map," shouted Drast in despair.

Pommel chuckled mirthlessly. "The world of the rude man differs from the polite man. What would Angeloff say if he renounced his vow now?"

Scratching his freckled cheeks Drast sighed. "Why did he take a vow of silence?"

"Many thought Angeloff was a terrorist—but he abhorred silence. He was a man of letters and he addressed a great many to the parliamentary building. He was arrested and sent to prison where he could not write letters. When he departed prison, the world had changed. After a targeted campaign of disinformation, Angeloff dissented from the dissenters. He was called a racist and a liar and was cast out from the revolutionary underground. This broke his heart more than anything else. He admitted that prison had saved him; whereas betrayal at the hands of his fellow thinkers was too much to take. He came to believe that it was absurd to think that any good would come from his words. He then retired from the sonic world."

"He must have known he was set up?" said Drast as he drew his habit around him.

"Prometheus created the first man who was called Phaenon," replied Pommel quickly. "He was well-liked and became Jupiter. When Prometheus tried to replicate his experiment, he failed to produce anything apart from evil beings. When he heard that Zeus would flood the world,

Prometheus went around warning his sons. One of his sons, Deucalion, whispered the truth about what was going to happen to some stones before fleeing the world. Then after the flood had dissipated these stones became the people from whom the human race descended." His sarcastic eyes were set alight by the fire and his button nose glistened. "We are the stones before the flood. First, the flood must come. Then from us must come—the future."

Angeloff's hairy legs began to move under the habit. They lifted him as he stood up and walked stiffly towards the wagon. "Where the fuck is *he* going?" asked Drast.

"The time has come to grab your rocks," declared Pommel.

Angeloff stood before the covered wagon where he knocked twice and waited politely.

"You've got your whole life to be a pain in the ass," said Honza on the other side. "Why don't you take tonight off?"

Standing with the locomotion of a Greek statue, Angeloff watched as the door creaked open. Inside the Maestro, the Bearded Lady, the Strongman, and the Astrologer stared at him.

"We know you can't talk," began the Astrologer. "You can't fool us."

The Strongman laughed tiredly. "He's got more hot hair than Honza."

"I'm sorry I'm *not* sorry," came the voice from the bunk. Then Honza's face appeared. "It looks like some village lost its prizewinning idiot."

Rearranging his straight line of observed silence into a pleasant smile, Angeloff cleared his throat and started talking. "I've been learning my lines and I've reached some conclusions that I would like to share with you," he explained with the confidence and rigour of a lecturer. "I don't think *Othello* is a racist play; rather, much of what has been written about *Othello* is racist. The standard reading of *Othello* is that he's a brute who's more beast than man: something like a Moorish Macbeth. This means that Othello is a primeval man who lacks humanity and that therefore the play is about a kind of primeval jealousy. The problem with this reading is that it bears no resemblance to what happens in the play. Othello is a brilliant man whose trust in others is so Christ-like in its completeness that when Iago so much as suggests that things are not what they seem; that Desdemona has fornicated with his confidante, his world is destroyed and he is driven mad. But this madness is not in the tradition of *Hamlet* whose main character pretends to be mad so as to prevent himself from falling into that madness which he is pretending. On the contrary, Othello is driven mad and thenceforth his actions are rational and not because he is primitive-and-jealous but because he is brilliant-but-mad. By way of comparison, *Othello* is as much a play about jealousy as *The Merchant of Venice* is about Shylock. It would be wrong to say that Othello does not suffer jealousy during the play. The distinction is that he is driven to jealousy by Iago and not by some instinctual jealousy that is merely a part of his alleged primitive nature. The play is about deception because Othello's sense of broken trust dominates the space where empathetic enquiry would otherwise solve the situation: an inquisitiveness that is a part of Othello's nature but one from which he has been cut off because of his newly minted madness." He took a deep breath. "Furthermore, *Othello* is not written to a standard where critical interpretations of the play can be undertaken."

"Amen," declared Honza.

"The text is not so meritorious that readers can interpret the motives of characters, and how these motives relate to the plot. And we have proof of this external to the play."

"We do?" asked the Astrologer as she lifted her jaw off the ground.

"What is the best version of *Othello*? The best version of the play is the film that was written and directed by Orson Welles. Welles ignored the source text almost entirely and wrote original material instead. In other words, it's the best *Othello*, because it is the least *Othello*."

The Maestro nodded off and muttered sweet nothings: "Sex education in this country is so bad you'd think the teachers would have the decency to teach them how to tie nooses…"

In the meantime, downstairs, the brothel had packed up for the night and the prostitutes and the occasional client snored, sniffled, or coughed. Stepping quietly over people's legs and avoiding shadows cast by the night watch candles Yulia tiptoed past colleagues and matriarchs. She made sure that she had her knife and her water satchel. She tightened her belt around her military trousers and began the journey to find the man that she loved.

DAY THREE

Opening his eyes on the chaise-longue, Fibber rolled onto the ground. His descent was backgrounded by chittering outside of the tent.

"Timofey, give me those matches," whispered Pavel outside.

"Whoops," muttered Timofey as the matches tinkled on the ground, "the damn thing opened—"

"Give it here!" Pavel scratched a match, holding it against the fabric. Silence was replaced by crackling and then heat replaced chill.

"Would you look at that?" approved Timofey.

"Move, you bastard!"

Fibber listened to their scuffling feet as he watched the flame inside the tent. Gripping a tankard of water, he chucked the thing against the material. He sighed and wondered why every morning had to start with danger.

"Spoilsport," muttered Timofey outside.

"Let's try somewhere else," replied Pavel.

"Why don't we just drink?"

"Fine," agreed Pavel as he stole beer from an actuary's larder.

Shaking his head in dismay Fibber inspected the leftovers: a pan of half-eaten prawn risotto and a half-finished bottle of red wine.

"A doctor's job is never finished," muttered Fibber as he filled a dirty plate with risotto. He then filled the same tankard with sour wine and sat down to enjoy his improvised breakfast. "We know that faith begins and ends with hope," he said as he forked risotto into his mouth. "Holiness is evidenced by love," he chewed, "because judgement begins and ends with holiness—" Coughing violently he spat the risotto onto the carpet where it splatted and bled. Then using sour wine, he washed out his mouth and started watching a shape outside of the tent. The shape was not moving, but it was clearly a person. Fibber got up and opened a flap in the side of the tent, dragged the shape inside, and then tied the flap shut behind the static article.

The thing yawned, "Oh God...what time...is it?"

Fibber touched his lips. "Be quiet. You'll wake the others."

Squinting and rubbing her eyes, Yulia stood up. "I need you alive. I want to be next to you. But I can smell those prawns from here."

Fibber gave her a peck on the cheek after which he sat on the chaise-lounge.

"Harry Pavelfurt was an undergraduate when Wittgenstein's *Blue* and *Brown Books* were being passed around by nosy students," said Fibber sleepily as he gestured at the food. "He refused to read them because he hated the cult that surrounded Wittgenstein. When he was older, he regretted not reading the work of the greatest philosopher who ever lived—whilst he was still alive." He paused because he forgot what he was going to say. "I've regretted not seeing you much," he continued as he smiled. "God must be punishing me with sour wine..."

As she plucked edibles, Yulia shuffled towards the chaise-longue where she swivelled on her booted feet, bent her knees, and collapsed backwards onto the shiny material.

"I've passed in and out of life," she said as she gently squeezed the warm shape of his knee.

"You can't be transcendental. If that were the case, humanism wouldn't exist and you wouldn't have come after me," replied Fibber.

"You're a man of surprise—" She bit into a coarse cracker and felt for the cheese. "I didn't know you were French."

"I'm bloody-minded. The prawn risotto was good once upon a time."

Wiping crumbs off of her chin Yulia whispered: "Malark has gone with Jozlov."

"The minister?" He shrugged. "I say we let history deal with them."

"We ought to let Labriola deal with them. I think Malark is touched by the Holy Spirit. The minister may not care about this place but she wants to survive. An artist and a bureaucrat get together and cut through walls, concrete, and steel looking for the exit. It's only natural."

"It doesn't make sense, Jozlov being here...unless she ruffled parliament's feathers..." He could feel his heart pumping faster as he whined and noticed sweat glistening on his hands.

"Why are you up here, Fibber? You're not just on your rounds?"

"I know that Aristotle thought that potentiality was mostly biological: a different sort of potentiality stalks this place. I don't have any proof. There's something holy about these typewriters. If works of holiness are evidenced by love then there must be a lot of love here."

Tapping her boots together Yulia laughed. "Why do we *want* God to love us? If God's love and our love are different—that may cause problems. If God could only show love through pain, for example, then we'd get a nasty shock on our knees. Sorry, the euphemism was irresistible."

"Nonsense," replied Fibber. "It's like when you wake up but your tent's on fire. You put the fire out. You don't sit there asking questions." He gave her a peck on the cheek.

"The world needs some kind of spiritual shock therapy," prescribed Yulia.

Fibber took another swig from the tankard, turned it into a fountain, and regained his senses as he gave her words the consideration they deserved. "The typewriters; maybe that's their purpose," he mumbled. "But there's *Othello* too..."

"*What may you be? Are you good or evil?*" she quoted as she wiped her boot. "Here's another question: are you worrying about the play, or about the man?"

"I need to see a man about a play." Jumping onto his feet Fibber started stretching. "It's good to keep fit," he said as he performed a series of jumping jacks. He puffed out his cheeks, stretched again, and was breathing heavily when he touched his stomach. "I'm going to be sick."

As if on cue, Doctor Grinko appeared from behind the curtain. His otherwise mighty moustache was uncurled and sat like a broom brush upon his upper lip which quivered sadly.

"I suffered from indigestion. I had a dream that my mother was doing jumping jacks. Then I had a dream that I was a doctor," said Doctor Grinko as he massaged his temples.

"You are having a bad dream right now," said Fibber as he nodded to his friend. "A black man and a white prostitute broke into your tent and are about to have sex on the chaise-lounge—"

"That's bloody news to *me*," grumbled Yulia.

Moaning Grinko manipulated his moustache. "I am a doctor—am I not?"

"Someone get Jung in here and give this Grinko goon a latent dream reading," shouted Yulia dramatically so everyone could hear.

A few plots down, an ex-university lecturer sat up in his folding bed, stared at the cramped and dirty tent surrounding him, and peered at the books that his ex-colleagues had detested. Professor Nikolai Stavrogin, formerly a Carl Jung specialist at the University of ———, swung his feet over the side of the bed and blinked at his wife in the folding bed opposite. She brushed aside her hair as she opened her blue eyes. "What is it, Nikolai?" she asked hoarsely.

"It's nothing—" He put on his glasses. "It's just…something's not right…"

Back in Doctor Grinko's tent, Fibber caught his breath. "We're heading upstairs, Grinko. Thank you for the prawn risotto and the wine."

"Oh dear," replied Grinko as though his guest had said something different. "We're all invited to *Othello*...I thought we had another forty-eight hours. I can't stand theatre in the morning. It upsets my digestion...among other things."

Fibber and Yulia checked their pockets and then held hands. They entered the alley outside where they found a new sense of aimlessness.

Meanwhile, Grinko continued his protestations. "Or maybe theatre in the morning destroys the day's equilibrium...perhaps the dream ego is involved in some way... because my morning identity refutes the theatre like a stone refutes the water...but then we're all dreaming in one way or another..."

His son, Pavel, returned with a sweaty brow. "Morning, Papa. You didn't smell any burning by any chance this morning, did you?"

"No, no...it's the wind," replied Grinko. He realized that it was Saturday. He glanced at the bottle of morphine on the table.

Using the original architectural maps Malark and Minister Jozlov climbed through a sierra of piping. They squeezed past valves and crouched under cooling centres whose job it was to regulate temperatures. The journey proved to be an unwanted exercise for Minister Jozlov who supported herself on a multi-limbed branch of piping.

"Stop...I need a breather," she gasped.

Taking a break in a tiny metallic enclave the two travellers stared up at pipes that stretched into the ceiling. "I wonder if the sun will rise," said Malark. "Then it dawns on me."

Rolling her eyes, Jozlov caught her breath. "You can tell this place is fishy from examining the plans. Have you ever seen the Rhind Papyrus? It's one of the earliest Egyptian mathematical texts. It's named after a Scotsman but never mind that circumstantial rubbish. The Rhind Papyrus was six metres long and dated from 1650 B.C. We generally understand the Egyptians were sophisticated mathematicians. But everyone lost their hats when they saw how the Rhind Papyrus only dealt with simple arithmetic. They didn't think it was for children, obviously..." She sniggered and then sneezed violently into a puff of steam. "The Rhind Papyrus was compounded by how the Egyptians didn't use place-value notation, decimal points, multiplication, division, plus, minus; or the number zero. Can you imagine an entire civilization without the number zero? *Without nothing?* We have the arrogance to think our mathematics are superior—even when they managed to build the Pyramids. We think the Tectum is more sophisticated than the Pyramids. But it lacks the beauty of the Pyramids." She shuddered and stopped herself from sneezing. "This place gives me the creeps."

A jet of steam shot over Malark's beret as he regained consciousness. "According to your estimations, we're running out of time." He nodded. "We need to move."

"Enough of the past...onto the future." Malark and Jozlov hobbled past pipework and walkways smelling of combustion, their paces shortening as the walkway narrowed. The walkway gave way to a compact space. "You're not a fan of state painters," noted Jozlov as she examined the map. "Tarkovsky and German are the ones they teach at the academy."

"Tarkovsky's oil paintings are sloppy because he's a mediocre draughtsman," replied Malark with the authority of a financial auditor. "As for German—I've never seen a painter so disgusted with paintings. I can imagine that's why your lot fancied him," he scoffed.

"I am here," she reminded him.

They forged ahead, rounded a corner, and entered a cavern where they found some others who had had the same idea. Kosha and three other furnace workers—Garo, Ruslanova, and Mashnaya—carried hydrogen lamps and excavated a wall. Malark noticed Kosha's goggles but he hadn't met the other three furnace workers. Garo was a woman of small build whose calves were the size of boulders. She wore an orange boiler suit, aluminium boots, and sharp gloves with painted-red tips. Ruslanova was a tall woman with close-cropped blonde hair. She was wearing a purple boiler suit, rubber boots, and a kind of metal cap that covered her head. Mashnaya, the other man, was in his undershirt and carrying the map. He wore a furry hat with wingtips that jutted out. He sweated harshly and refused to wear anything else.

"Kosha," said Malark gleefully.

"Deputy…" The foreman's tone was professional. "We're doing routine repair work. Each one of us is Hercules and these are our labours."

"There's no work for you down here."

"I could say the same about you, deputy."

"My jurisdiction knows no frame. There's not a single square inch of concrete in this fucking thing that nips by without my scrutiny." He sucked in silence and then he sighed. "Kosha, are you trying to break out too?"

"Ruslanova reminded me that the Tectum was a head," came the conceited answer. "We are drawing an analogy between brains and machinery. We have a limited under-standing of mental mechanics but we have tasked ourselves with getting to the bottom of this obsolete psychological notion," he added with a sign of weariness and an expecta-tion of swift death.

"Why don't we join forces?" asked Minister Jozlov as though she was the eternal child at the back of the classroom.

The foreman was tired of bureaucrats. "What do *you* want?"

"I want to leave this building…which is what *you* want."

Kosha paused. "Why don't *you* take this pickaxe and kill that bastard wall?

Disappointed by the reciprocal action that involved her doing the work, Jozlov gripped the pickaxe and attacked the wall.

Detaching his goggles, Kosha stared at Malark. "If we knock through this wall, we'll have base camp right under our noses. That's our hypothesis, anyway."

"Kosha's crazy and he *nose* it," replied Malark.

"We noticed the shape of the Tectum when we arrived. We drafted a series of maps using Euclidean geometry and the occasional Eulerian graph."

Malark swallowed, "This is the best exit you could find?"

"We used Euler's solution to plot a walk around Königsberg where he had to cross seven bridges and then get back to where he started. We've just witnessed the birth of graph extension, Malark, and *boy* is it painful…"

Through the combined might of Jozlov, Mashnaya, Ruslanova, and Garo, the wall was breached and showed a passage to the huge chamber next door.

"Shit," said Ruslanova. "It worked."

The sun came alive on the horizon and the wooden shed shrunk in the sun's rays. Standing outside of the shed was Melker. He watched the hogs devouring Agapov's corpse as though it were a gigantic popsicle of blood. Exiting the house, Marina came to stand by Melker where she patted him on the back, check her pulse, and rub her hands for warmth. "Melker…?"

"Mama…why are you and Mama living…out here?"

Sighing Marina removed her hand from his back. "The writer Pyotr Gerchakov…have you heard of him?"

"He's like a patron saint for dissident writers. I can't remember the last novel he wrote because it was years ago," replied Melker excitedly. "It was the size of a tombstone and satirized everything. It was the most radical thing ever written—then he disappeared…"

Nodding politely Marina smiled awkwardly. "*I'm* Pyotr Gerchakov," she declared. "Forced out here against my own will. I never used my own name for writing." She chuckled. "I made George Eliot look like the male chauvinist she was."

"But that means...you're illegal...you're public enemy number one!"

Patting him again on the back she sniggered and craned her neck back. "I don't listen to silly things people say about me."

"Why...weren't you shot?"

"They wanted to shoot me; then they devised a superior punishment. When you kill a writer, you martyr them and people want to read their books; when you keep a writer alive, however, and prevent them from working—they starve."

The snow squeaked as Melker shifted his weight. "But you *hate* books."

"I do...but I love you, Melker...and your mother."

Now roused she recited,

And if without certainty we
Fumble with eternity
Telling us it told us so when
First deduction whispered back then
Shrug off the buckling corporation
Laugh down the tutor's fornication
With a gadfly nip empiricism
Itch a gladly bitter scepticism.
But against the question lipping is God
There is a fear we richen that is flawed

A tulip we reckon spreads at beck
And call—but we cannot think a dog sane.
When ice no longer is, ice becomes
Supple, doggies swim, and pogroms
Are boated to peaceful lands
Whilst men, exempt, wash their hands.

The wasteland whispered as her words trailed off. She smiled and was lost for words to follow those which she had spoken. For the first time, Melker began to admire his mother. He looked at the hogs, regretted watching the human popsicle, and then looked back at Marina. "You don't want to write?" he asked. "Because you *could*. I promise I wouldn't tell—"

"Don't be silly," she replied as an upper left arm was carried away by a lucky piglet.

Re-applying his goggles, Kosha dangled his hydrogen lamp in front of the cavity. In rushed a foggy odour that addled the minds of the runaway group who all pinched their noses and wept.

"The chamber of *stank*," complained Jozlov as her eyes watered and she considered quitting.

"The reek of death," Kosha corrected.

Malark peered over his shoulder to investigate the crypt-like remains of the construction site. The shortfall of light allowed dark shapes to shroud themselves like bleak rows of gravestones aligning with an adjacent row of monuments. Extracting a sheet of paper from her pocket, Ruslanova folded the paper into an airplane. She taped a match to its side, lit the match, and launched the paper airplane through the cavity. The airplane cast light on an abandoned construction office whose windows had been shattered with copper bullets, queues of mummi-fied bodies, discarded machinery, and medieval scaffold-ing erected from sloppily cut timber tied together using ribbons of ripped clothing. The maiden flight of thirty seconds culminated in the airplane crashing into an old earthmover.

"The dead building nothing—not even memories," said Kosha as he discerned a walkway through the site to the far side of the wall.

The expedition entered the dank space. "We'll bump into Sabala and Syama down here," Kosha added with shud-dering shoulders. "The dogs of the underworld who guard Kalichi: those pooches will round us up and apply their final judgement to our bottoms..."

Malark ignored the loopy fellow leading them. "Which way?"

"There's too much noise, mathematically speaking," replied Mashnaya as he scanned the map brightened by the burning dazzle of the shakily held hydrogen lamps. "The place was left in a hurry. They sealed the exit using concrete and bodies." He looked up. "This way..."

Discerning a hydrogen lamp dangling underneath his nose, Malark took the lamp from Garo. Then she went to pass one to Minister Jozlov. She faltered, however, and kept the lamp.

Minister Jozlov sighed as she and the others followed Mashnaya over the rocky terrain. The path he chose was dotted with high-visibility migrants whose bodies had atrophied. Counting the untold corpses, the runaway group concluded that the level of death was impressive.

Tapping Mashnaya's shoulder, Ruslanova scoffed. "You breathe like you're inside a radio."

"The air is thick," he explained as he stopped before a heap of corpses. They had been gunned down at the last moment and appeared to be clawing at something that might have postponed death. "It's a moon-gate," noted Mashnaya. The hole had been patched up with concrete. "If we make a start, we'll be out of here in no time," he said hopefully.

"Why hasn't anyone thought of doing what we're doing?" asked Jozlov.

"You didn't know before you found us," replied Kosha.

"We're hardly an army," she said. "Why are the rest of them upstairs?"

Malark laughed. "They don't cherish the world as we do, minister." He showed his light around the space, highlighting mummified bodies as he went. "Deconstruction aims to overcome hidden privileges that intellectuals use to suppress the masses. The people upstairs have a world made of privileges that are not their own. They are cut off from this planet," he explained as he propped his boot upon a boulder. "For centuries our ancestors colonized the world's wastelands—but the uncolonized land today is that of the human mind." He whistled as he looked around the construction site. "I haven't thought about painting since I blackmailed you into removing your clothes."

Ruslanova and Garo looked at each other.

Kosha coughed. "We've no time for tittle-tattle." He nodded at the map pleasantly. "Mashnaya says that we'll be out of here in no time if we start now. No politician has ever admitted this—but counsel is worth every penny."

"I get paid shit," laughed Mashnaya.

"Give me the pickaxe," said Minister Jozlov. She pushed away the corpses; she could have sworn that some of them she knew. She thought that she recognized the faces—even though their features were wholly unrecognizable. Aiming her pickaxe, she chinked the blade on the concrete. Another thrust sprayed dust through the beams of the hydrogen lamps. "Pacific Islanders thought that the world was on the back of a cosmic turtle: they called it Bedawang," she explained as she dug her pickaxe into the wall. "There were two snakes that covered his back and a black stone that covered the underworld. We've got Malark and Kosha—I've no intention of the being the black stone," she added.

For a moment Ruslanova thought that Minister Jozlov was racist.

"We don't want you to be the hatch over the underworld," assured Kosha. "I can assure you that it's not better being a snake."

Her pickaxe delivered a chunk of concrete. "On paper, I'm the most important person here. If anything cocks up, you can bet that it will be *my* problem." She feigned a cry of horror. "I'll be shoving my pearly cheeks through the breached hull as the iceberg cuts through." Another chunk of concrete was ejected by the minister's brave pickaxe. "Open you bastard!"

"The minister was a historian until she realized there was no future in it," said Malark.

"Who wants Malark to be the black stone if things go pear-shaped?" asked Kosha.

The other furnace workers raised their hands and wiped sweat from their foreheads.

Jozlov raised her pickaxe and delivered another blow to the wall. The furnace workers raised their pickaxes, targeted the remaining plug of the moon gate, and chipped away quickly.

Meanwhile, Malark propped his pickaxe on his shoulder. "It's the month of January and Vladimir Lenin is on his deathbed. Joseph Stalin is sitting there next to him and Lenin asks him, *How will you lead Russia when so many people refuse to follow you?* And Stalin smiles and replies, *Don't worry…anyone who doesn't follow me will follow you…*"

Malark lifted his pickaxe and plunged it into the wall. A thousand dead bodies watched, happy to see someone exercising the half-chance which they had been denied.

Broaching the moss-covered staircase, Fibber and Yulia ascended to the fourth floor. The staircase wound towards another flight of steps at the top of which was a feathered boy who sported a beaked mouth and yellow legs. Encroached by books from every angle, he was holding one in his feathery hands. Suddenly, the feathery youth looked up from his book and said, "Doubtless Thomas Jefferson would have struggled to describe the level of hypocrisy upstairs."

"Hyppolite spent his time translating Marx into French," replied Fibber as he inspected the impromptu library surrounding him. "He wrote two books on logic and Hegel."

"You tried to impress me by recalling authors by memory...but the two things you mentioned are unconnected and you know it." He squinted. "Shame on you, Overseer."

Glancing at Yulia for a second, Fibber propped his boot up on a step. "I want to try out for the play," he lied as harshly as he breathed. "Why do you think that I'm the Overseer?"

"You have the pretence of authority and you smell. I shall leave the connection to you and your venerable friend." He returned to his book. "You mentioned the play," he said without looking up.

"Yes?"

"They have cast Othello. If you were the Overseer, you would have known that." He looked up from his book. His eyes flicked between them. "Who are you?"

"A very tired man." Fibber tightened his bootstraps. He eyed the feathery backside.

Yulia grabbed Fibber's jacket and yanked him backwards. "You'll go woozy down there. Too much oxygen and not the good kind," she said evasively.

"They have forged ahead without me," lamented Fibber.

"I knew they would. It's people like them who can't tell the difference between voluntary and involuntary euthanasia."

"I couldn't have put it better myself," cheered the Chicken Boy. "I am travelling to the world of Zadie Smith and have no intention of returning before things improve immeasurably."

Yulia realized why Fibber had tightened his straps when he propelled himself upwards and then pushed open the huge doors. Following him through the doors, Yulia felt her brain succumb to an imperceptible confusion as though she had cracked open to the middle of a very long Polish novel, refused to learn the language, and then decided to count all the diacritics.

Drast and Pommel played guitar flamenco-style as toga-wearing actors performed across an elevated stage, moving inelegantly over squeaky boards, and looking miserable.

"These letters poppadom, Iago, to the pilot," delivered Honza who had a habit of exchanging verbs for foods. "And by him, cheesecake my duties to the senate. That done, I will be frosting on the works, celery there to me—"

"Well, my good lord, I'll do it," replied Angeloff who had risen to the challenge of playing Iago.

"This fortification, gentlemen, shall we noodle it?"

They exited as Drast and Pommel abandoned their guitars. They repositioned cut-outs of vineyards after which they released a roll of astro-turf and returned embarrassingly backstage.

The Bearded Lady, the Strongman, and the Astrologer appeared as Desdemona, Cassio, and Emilia, respectively.

"I am a stereotype," recited the Bearded Lady who wished to remind his audience of the nature of his character.

"Be thou assured, good Cassio, I will do all my abilities in thy behalf."

"Good madam, do. I warrant it grieves my husband as if the cause were his," replied the Astrologer.

"I am a stereotype but that's an honest fellow. Do not doubt, Cassio, that I am a stereotype, but I will have my lord and you again as friendly as you were."

"BOUNTEOUS MADAM WHATEVER SHALL BECOME OF CASSIO HE'S NEVER ANYTHING BUT YOUR TRUE SERVANT," screamed the Strongman.

"I am a stereotype. I know it. Thank you. You do love my lord. You have known him long; and be you well assured he shall, in strangeness, stand no farther off than in politic distance." The Bearded Lady rolled his eyes.

Casting his eyes to the imaginary audience the Strong-man choked. "Christ!"

Jumping out of his director's chair, the Maestro shook his copy of *Othello*. He stomped around in circles, swore at everyone, and gave the entire cast the middle-finger. "You have one job," he shouted vehemently. "Deliver your god-damn lines to the best of your ability!" Noticing that every-one was staring over his head, the Maestro turned around and frowned powerfully. "We're closed today. Who are you?"

"I'm the Overseer," replied Fibber.

"*Fuck*—!" The Maestro tripped over his chair, held his kneecaps in pain, and wandered over to the Overseer and his companion. "He's adorable!" he said of the Overseer. "He's turned out to be an absolute beauty! Let me extend a warm welcome, too, to his lady-friend who galvanizes the steel of the Overseer who demonstrates that we should discard madness and embrace sanity." He clasped his hands together and fluttered his eyelashes. "We meet our sublime collaborator who outshines the great Malark himself—his deputy, no less…"

He farted.

"The Overseer is the God of wisdom; he was born from the light of Buddha's head and he has more accolades than the Indian kings." He laughed nervously, gathering his syntax. "The version that I would like to experience is where the Overseer converts hundreds to Buddhism on the Earth and then does the same when he descends to the depths of the ocean." He clapped his hands and nodded persuasively. "You are the founder of green branches!" Thudding before him, Yulia tapped his cheek with her forefinger. "If you gave a damn about Buddhism then you would know that we're all potential Buddhas. That God of wisdom, Manjushri, holds a book as well as a sword. Fibber bears less resemblance to him than you do."

"Overseer," whined the Maestro, "she doesn't have our peculiar bond!"

"I know the book…but which is the sword?" asked Fibber.

"The sword stares through us," laughed Yulia.

Fibber clomped next to Yulia where he observed the Maestro's unzipped trousers. Whimpering in embarrassment, the Maestro zipped up his fly and exhaled through pursed lips.

"I would have put the pornographic *Othello* past you. But that's common in our modern society," Fibber said as he slapped his hand's hand on the Maestro's shoulders. "If your blood is in the Rh group then I'm preparing myself to forgive you. Because you greeted us with mythological trash, I'm going to return the favour. Churchwomen…strum your guitars."

Drast and Pommel, who were making tea, stopped, and looked at each other. They picked up their guitars and strummed Latin chords that stung the room with deflated sex appeal.

Yulia covered her ears. "Stop playing!" she said. "You sound like ecofeminists! It's all very well to make a connection between human domination over nature and male domination over women. We need to define what we mean by domination—because by pulling the ecofeminist line we're towing the Christian line that human beings are outside of nature."

The two habited figures sighed, lowered their guitars, and resumed making tea.

"If we intend to keep the Overseer exterior to this production then we ought to get to the bottom of what the play is about," stated Yulia bluntly. "Shock therapy drives the play. Iago shocks Othello into madness after telling him about betrayals that are too close to home."

The floorboards creaked as the Astrologer folded her arms and wagged her head.

"Individualism was once the greatest power in the world. It has turned to madness, now, and has driven people mad," warned Yulia as the Maestro stared at her. "The only option open to saving everyone is a form of spiritual shock therapy.

An action, or series of events that will shock the world into empathy and therefore destroy the individualistic madness that rules us."

"Dinkum oil!" Angeloff shouted as he produced a pair of scissors and cut his toga. The air of improvisation washed over his upper thigh and he vented a sigh of relief and victory.

Fibber's eyes widened. He pushed the Maestro out of the way as he clonked towards the stage where he reached out his hands. "A pair of scissors! May I borrow them?"

"I don't see why not," agreed Angeloff. He passed them down and watched the Overseer lower his trousers and then fumble desperately under his package.

"This Overseer is far out," whispered the Astrologer to the Strongman. "It's a good thing we're behind the Tectum's eyes. He can't see the naughtiness we're all getting up to…" Aiming blades under his crotch Fibber snipped twice, felt the pwang of free fabric, and straightened up with a look of divine appeasement on his face. "Who would have thought?"

The Maestro sneered. What a strange man, he thought.

"I would have changed my underwear if I had known the extent of my job," Fibber told Angeloff whose grey eyes contemplated the cheery relief of the Overseer. "Your name?"

"I sing for your thighs." There was a long pause. "My name is Angeloff, and—"

He was cut short when Fibber grabbed him and pulled him onto the ground. "Don't gargle beneath me," said Fibber as he held down the monkish figure on the ground and gurned. "I suspected who you were when you passed that weapon to me without instructing me in its use. I've trailed you ever since Marshall Volkov was crushed beneath those typewriters; now I find you playing the most odious villain to ever grace the stage. But your true character outshines the character of Iago with its blackness and baseness—!" Angeloff wished to speak but Fibber kept his thumb in his mouth. "You think I suffer from persecutory delusions but I'll have you know that poets *always* tell the truth!"

"Don't kill my Iago!" screeched the Maestro in the background.

"I'll put you in a cage like the Orson Welles movie!"

"*But I'm your father,*" declared Angeloff.

Loosening his grip on Angeloff's tongue Fibber paused. "I never knew my father."

"I've got your attention now." He caught his breath. "I'm not your father but I have something to say to you. Pyotr Gerchakov."

"If you're Gerchakov then God is drunk. We have a drunk God!"

"I am *not* Gerchakov…what do you know of him?"

"In the underground everyone knew that he was a genius." His eyes hardened. "Did you help the Bluebloods destroy *Despotism's Isle?*"

"I helped…to publish…the damn thing," gasped Angeloff. Gawping around the fourth floor, Fibber searched for God. "And he is a *she,*" Angeloff continued. "They send dissidents to the wasteland and she was no exception. She forced my vow of silence upon me."

"Have you any proof?" asked Fibber.

Hoisting the contents of his toga Angeloff visited his rucksack.

"I didn't have time to smuggle it out before the book went to print...the last paragraph of *Despotism's Isle...*" He extracted a notebook and pulled out a piece of paper.

Angeloff handed the paper to Fibber, who delivered the words with reverence.

> In a word, I've been lucky;
> Others and Angeloff rescue.
> In this novel, it struck me
> That empathy's unknown hue
> Is never green, never true
> For, the thought that things are true
> Ought not be for me, or you.
> I'm tickled to think of fate
> On farms—many things to do.

The vents above rippled the scrap in Fibber's fingers. Examining the words for a second time he ignored the rehearsal that he and his lover had interrupted. "You think he's a terrorist?" complained Honza. "He drinks tea and reads poetry with those two jackasses. You're wrong."

"We've been lied to," whispered Fibber.

Angeloff looked at Yulia. "You mentioned shock therapy...I had the same idea...if we all have the same idea there must be some truth in what we think?"

"That's what the Overseer's worried about," replied Yulia sadly.

"Looking at that jacket I'd say you got the wrong idea," said Honza, who groaned.

Malark and Minister Jozlov, along with Garo, Ruslanova, Kosha, and Mashnaya, attacked the wall using their pickaxes. Backlit by hydrogen lamps, chips of concrete shot through the air and cast thread-like shadows on the bodies of the dead. "Concrete cork," described Kosha as he wiped the dust from his eyebrows. Then Jozlov caught sight of something behind the wall. "Hold your pickaxes…" The wall gave way and their smiles were wiped away by mystery. They were looking at a diving-bell-shaped spheroid that had been left behind the wall. A series of fin-like borders ran along the surface of the object; there was no sign of decay and the machine signified a strange sort of life when Ruslanova held her hydrogen lamp close to it. "Syncretism," hiccupped Kosha as his face lowered. "How is that for a global scheme? It's probably a bomb with our luck. I don't suppose you know what makes it tick, minister?"

She was genuinely baffled. "I don't know anything about this thing. It was never on the plans we used when we built this place."

Ruslanova grunted as she held up her hydrogen lamp. "Old habits die hard."

"Clear this concrete away. But do it gently," suggested Kosha. Using their pickaxes as spoons they scraped away the remaining concrete surrounding the machine. The machine was large and powered by electricity. But there was no plug, Kosha noticed, and something like a heartbeat was coming from the centre of the machine. Using her hydrogen lamp Ruslanova showed an access panel.

"Do you have that screwdriver of yours?" asked Mashnaya.

Ruslanova removed the screwdriver from her pocket and handed it to Mashnaya. "Knock yourself out...what do you think, Garo?"

"You burn your hands when you touch the fire," promised Garo.

"If flames come out of that thing, they'll make the dragons blush!"

"We don't have many options," said Mashnaya.

"Speaking as your Deputy Overseer, I suggest that we move the bloody thing," Malark coughed as he squinted in the dark. "We already have enough people chewing scenery."

Kosha tapped Mashnaya's back: "Take a look..."

The metallic heartbeat increased when Mashnaya unscrewed the access panel. Examining the green interior Mashnaya discovered a branch-like system that operated through the pressure-controlled pumping of various fluids. He smiled because he was impressed.

Minister Jozlov thought she heard something. "What was that?"

Malark hesitated. "Where?"

"It was in the corner...I swear it."

"You are seeing things. You should get a job in politics," replied Malark. "Except you beat me to it."

"I've got it," said Mashnaya with a chest puffed with excitement, "it's a tree diagram!"

Jozlov flinched. Something was dripping on her. Condensation? Blood?

"We use tree diagrams to figure out the right action to take when every strategy has an uncertain outcome," explained Mashnaya. "There are square nodes that serve as decision nodes, and there are circular nodes that are random nodes; except the branches that leave the random nodes have *known probabilities*. What happens is that they reach a terminal node; if you look at every branch, they indicate the consequence of each terminal node." He paused. "Tree diagrams are simple...but I've never seen one this complex before."

"I'm glad you're here. Fuck a duck," laughed Malark.

Ruslanova pointed at the device that emitted the heartbeat. "Does that control the detonator?"

"Well-spotted, comrade." Winking in the darkness Mashnaya twiddled his fingers. "Any one of these branches could lead to the outcome with the highest gain...it's numerical...which suggests that somebody somewhere is converting observations into data..."

"Everyone's using typewriters. They've all got this compulsion," asserted Malark.

Kosha smirked. "If you worship inanimate objects then you will become like them. Christians have the arrogance to deny objects their divinity. But they think that pagans can't worship correctly. They can't accept that pagans worship without worshipping..."

"I think I've found the right branch," interrupted Mashnaya as he twisted the branch using the screwdriver, snapped the branch, and watched the fluid inside spurt everywhere. Sweat dripped down Mashnaya's forehead as the metallic heartbeat ceased and he relaxed. "What a brilliant piece of engineering," he approved. "The *bomb* wasn't too bad either."

"Hang about, it could still be dangerous!" said Kosha.

"It's quite harmless."

"*Quite harmless*," Malark satirised.

Watching the furnace workers drag the spheroid device to one side Malark imagined how large the crater would have been if the bomb had been allowed to complete its program. Suddenly a cool breeze flowed over them and Kosha's eyes were brightened by the exterior sunlight that beat down on the runaway group and their soiled architectural plans. Ruslanova enjoyed the fresh air. They had beaten the system, she thought.

"I was beginning to forget what it felt like," said Kosha.

Dazed by recent events, Melker decided to visit his favourite stream. In the meantime, his two mothers sat in the kitchen grinding mashed potatoes that would then be dehydrated into flour. "Let's see," said Marina as she ground her pestle against the side of the mortar, "what do I miss about the parliamentary district…"

"No doubt you miss the food," replied Olga. "Do you have to mention it?"

"No one takes the time to prepare their food anymore… not like you should. People ought to mutter about food as though they're muttering about sex."

"You mutter about indulgent trash."

"What's indulgent about chicken liver parfait?" She threw down her pestle. "And with oak moss and truffle toast; crab biscuits and red cabbage gazpacho; roast foie gras." Triumphant with the silence that she had inspired in her partner, Marina bobbed her head sagely. "I don't think food is vulgar; neither is food indulgent but the people who make it have to be. Much better to have an indulgent chef than a threadbare one who prays between preparations. They can't be creative without having the *potential* of vulgarity. Cabernet-braised short ribs," she said suddenly and with great affection. "For the marination, the parliamentary chef sliced off the excess fat and then chucked the ribs and a bottle of cabernet sauvignon into a bowl. He added celery, carrots, leeks, bay leaves, garlic, thyme, and salt and pepper. After marination, he rolled the ribs in flour, seared them, and baked them with the vegetables for three hours…"

"You are going to *die* if you keep on talking like this," said Olga.

Picking up her pestle, Marina returned to her potatoes. "Captain Gurkin will seek out that woman," she added surreptitiously. "We can't murder Gurkin. We can't rely on hogs."

"They don't care about people like Agapov," calmed Olga. "She won't be missed."

"You don't understand these bureaucrats," replied Marina. "They can't file the paperwork if they don't have the body." She breathed. "What are we going to *do*?"

Olga listened to the wind lapping at the window. "We could leave here," she said.

"And go where?"

"The black forest."

"No shortage of bear meat," replied Marina. "The bears won't be vegetarian." She banged the table with her fist. "We're tangled up! Hopelessly tangled up!

"We are *not* tangled up."

"You'd have to be mad to think that. How does charity serve the survivalist? That woman's back was on the snow... he should have left her to starve or freeze to death..."

"I'm sorry I saved your life—"

"I don't think we'll ever know," came the reply as the amount of potato flour increased.

Meanwhile, a mile away, Melker was lying in the snow. His arms were twisted beneath him and he was riddled with bullet holes.

As he listened to the stream, Captain Gurkin smoothed his semi-automatic weapon. Hastily, he turned and trudged back to his raid tank which was nestled in the recently fallen snow.

Surrounding the raid tank were tattered men smoking cigarettes, listening for orders, and cursing the numbing weather. They wore makeshift armour made from scrap metal. The boots they wore had holes in them and their eyes were dreary holes sucking in the empty landscape. A petite, bearded man who was wearing a winter coat, fingerless gloves, and a pince-nez was holding an equally tattered radio set. He jutted out his lower lip and called for Captain Gurkin. "In the Tectum," exclaimed the radio operator. "Some busy body ruined the bomb!"

For a split second Gurkin was strained, exhausted, and crackbrained. "It's started. Let's move," he commanded; then cigarettes stained the snow and the air was filled with fumes.

Around the city, some farms produced grain and sometimes meat when laboratories could not meet the demands of parliament. One of the farms was a ramshackle building that was owned by an older woman who had once been a major landowner in the city; now reduced to nurturing grain and livestock, she was allowed the privilege of sending her daughter to the local university. The daughter was in her teens and was an unfussy person with light skin. That day she was wearing military attire and sitting in the kitchen as her mother cooked silently. Reading *Despotism's Isle,* she sat in a Brunswick-green armchair waiting for the forthcoming campaign in which she and other peasants would go to battle with Plum Lukum's forces.

There was a knock at the door. The Student hid *Despotism's Isle* under a throw pillow and went to open the front door.

Outside people and machines were rumbling behind the outline of a grizzled soldier who was wearing nothing more than copper boots, combat-green trousers, and a white undershirt. A spear was slung over his shoulder, and his lips were uneasy and quivering.

"Roll call," he said wretchedly. "Men and women to their animals…"

The Student matter-of-factly nodded, kissed her wordless mother goodbye, picked up her rucksack, and marched through the doorway to fasten herself to the cheap army. The Student joined the muster parade on horseback and rode alongside the army that stretched for miles in both directions; there were donkeys, motorbikes, and horse-drawn carts. The occasional raid tank subdued this civilian army, armed with spears, rifles, and sharpened toothbrushes.

A horse-drawn cart caught between a raid tank and motorbikes carried men who removed their caps at the sight of the Student.

She asked them, "How far away is the battle?"

"This one follows the law!" replied the Drinker who relaxed his bottle of whiskey. Thin and despondent, the Drinker was in his forties and his feet were swollen in ankle-length boots. He had a long nose, distended with abuse, plastic chain mail, cotton gloves, and a helmet. "A great many miles to go...what do you think of our line of suicides?"

"Nothing else will put an end to Plum Lukum's reign of terror," clarified the Student.

"We're all starring in *The Mother Of Us All*. Who wants to be Susan B. Anthony?" He shook his head. "Why did Gertrude Stein write a libretto? That's what I want to know..."

"You must think this is the Bible, then," said the Student.

"Barnabas fancied that burnt offerings and sacrifices were of no use to the Lord...if that position's good enough for Barnabas, then it's good enough for me...this mega-sacrifice will bankrupt the country...fighting for peace is like fucking for virginity."

Kicking her horse's ribcage, the Student galloped a hundred metres hence.

Watching her departure, the Drinker tapped the driver's helmet: "You're driving this limousine...why don't you speed up? This velocity-challenged crate refuses to keep up! What's the use of soldiering if we can't give young people a hard time?"

"You bastard," said the driver as he whipped reigns half-covered in snow. He wore a stovepipe hat, a leather jerkin, and Wellington boots. "They'll put you at the front with bayonets and garlic."

"Fat chance...I'll find some mushrooms and make a stew. Beats riding *this* thing..." The Drinker was drowned out by the splattering mud, clinking armour, and singing soldiers as another horse-drawn cart pulled up alongside and crushed field mice under its wooden wheels. Meanwhile, ten drunk soldiers danced in a line, kicking their legs like vain showgirls; a greyish woman wearing a purple fez played an accordion and kept time with her foot.

Plum Lukuuuuuum!
Sweet death, what is your tune?
Will it make me sweet, make me sick?
Cut my hair, give me a stick
To beat—to beeeeeat—the politicians!

Plum Lukuuuuuum!
Belgian Queen, where's my tomb?
Will I sleep alone, with a girl?
Under filth, my hair in curls
For strangling—strangliiiiiing—politicians!

Unbeknownst to the singing and dancing soldiers, Captain Gurkin's raid tank had pulled alongside their horse-drawn cart. Private Rakovsky aimed his semi-automatic pistol as Captain Gurkin shouted: "I'll see every one of you court-martialled and hanged! Do you understand?"

Rakovsky shot through the Drinker's bottle: glass and whiskey sprayed everywhere. "That was medicinal. I need my medicine," wept the Drinker.

"You need one warning," was Gurkin's shouted reply. He tapped the raid tank and the vehicle chugged ahead leaving the horse-drawn carts in the squelching mud.

A combination of tobacco smoke and diesel suffused Gurkin's thoughts. As he pondered how they had learnt that song, a collected human consciousness became believable.

In the meantime, Fibber and Yulia recoiled as they watched *Othello*'s infamous Act Five, Scene Two, as performed by the thespian might of the Metaphysical Circus— and Honza. Requiring a ladder on which to play the scene correctly, Honza balanced himself precariously and delivered his lines as best as possible under food-related circumstances: "I macaroni, amen."

"And have you mercy too on my stereotype?" replied the Bearded Lady. "I never did offend you in my life, never loved Cassio but with such general warranty of heaven as I might love. I never gave him token because I am a stereotype!"

"By heaven, I toasted my handkerchief in his hand. O perjured woman, thou dost cranberry my heart and mak'st me cannoli what I intend to do a carrot which I thought a sacrifice. I buttered the handkerchief."

"He found it then. I never gave it to him. Send for him hither. Let him confess the truth because I am a stereotype."

"He hath porked!" Honza winced.

Fibber watched between his fingers but Yulia came to enjoy the show.

The Maestro approved of neither reaction and covered his face with his hands too, he also pressed his thighs together and wept quietly.

e w"What, my lord?" asked the Bearded Lady. "I cannot hear because I am a stereotype."

"That he has porked thee!"

"How? Unlawfully? Stereotypically?"

Doing a double-take Honza then flapped his hands. "Well, yeah."

"He will not say so."

"Pumpkin, strumpet!"

"O, banish my stereotype, my lord, but kill my stereotype not!"

"Courgette! Strumpet!" Honza shouted as he fetched a pillow from a pre-arranged string tied to the ladder on which he was standing.

The Bearded Lady demanded, "Kill my stereotype tomorrow, let me live tonight! But while I say one prayer!"

"It's too late!" declared Honza. He put the pillow on the Bearded Lady's face.

Some time passed.

"*I can't breathe*," muttered the Bearded Lady.

Suddenly, the Strongman appeared onstage and kicked the ladder off of its feet. Thinking he might take flight, Honza regrettably struck the ground with a violent thud.

Honza spat out some sawdust. "What the hell's wrong with you?"

The Maestro coughed in dismay, stood up from his deck-chair, and dropped his jaw. "Cassio! What are you doing?"

"But doesn't Cassio—?" Opening his script to the right page the Strongman squinted. "I thought...no...no...you're right."

Honza rolled his eyes. "Don't be ashamed of yourself. That's your mother's job."

"Take a break," lamented the Maestro whose back bowed like a limp noodle. "For God's sake...I might as well open a novelty museum with stuffed frogs." He glowered at Fibber and Yulia who returned polarized expressions that summarized the whole performance. "When Scarlatti wanted to stage Goldoni's *Le Donne di Buon Unore,* he composed the music whilst Massine did the choreography. They called the opera, *The Good-Humoured Ladies.*"

Nodding sadly, Fibber thought vaguely of escape.

"I'm directing a terrible version of *The Good-Humoured Ladies,*" concluded the Maestro, "about to become *The Bad-Humoured Director.*"

"The problem is that you are directing a bad *Othello,*" replied Yulia.

The Maestro had a quizzical look. "I thought you enjoyed it."

"I revelled in its wrongness," Yulia said as Fibber bulged his eyes and stifled a giggle. "If God refuses to prevent this play, then God must be impotent. But if God is able—but merely lacks the will…then God is *malevolent*." She nodded to herself as the Maestro winced. "We have a third option: if God is both able *and* willing to stop this play, then what in the name of God enables you to continue? Thus, we have a right to fear things that we do not understand."

The Maestro snivelled.

"We have to figure out whether this *Othello* is natural evil; or moral evil," assumed Fibber. "Was it born from nature; or from evil people?" He winked at the Maestro.

"Why do you ask simple questions?" complained Yulia.

"It's not simple…because if we assume this play is a natural evil then it may have its uses. It may be a force for *good*."

"You won't forget the third evil, will you?"

"A disproportion between virtue and happiness; vice and misery; the wicked prosper but the virtuous suffer. Desdemona indeed suffers a grim fate despite her own virtuosity. But we could say the same for Othello."

"It can't be that bad if you got all this from it," chirped the Maestro.

"But art shouldn't always make people think," replied Yulia.

"Time to pack up and go to bed," said Fibber. "Can we sleep in the circus tent?"

The Maestro tensed. "…*Yes*."

"I gave that bird-boy instructions that he should bar the exit. We can't have you absconding like some Blueblood accountant." He tapped the Maestro's cheek.

As Fibber and Yulia strolled towards the circus tent, the Astrologer caught up with them, stopped before them, panting, and demanded to talk to the Overseer.

Fibber stopped. "What?"

"We've heard how everyone is typing downstairs. Is that true?"

"Where are yours?"

"They're here...but we—"

"You *have* to type...we have targets," Fibber said.

Yulia pulled him inside of the circus tent and they both recoiled at the appalling stench. Perhaps this was why the Strongman and the Astrologer slept in their own tent, Fibber thought.

Meanwhile, the Astrologer returned to the stage where the Strongman complimented her costume. She waved him down like a falcon and gave him a peck on the cheek.

"What was that for?" asked the Strongman.

"For being you...here and now."

"I will always be here...we will always be here," said the Strongman, who felt unwell.

Outside the wind increased and broken snowfalls patrolled the distance and sometimes the foreground. A depression grew at the base of the Tectum until suddenly the earth gave way. Fingers emerged from the undergrowth and patches of grass and dirt were dispersed in the air. An arm appeared and then an entire body wormed its way onto the surface.

"We're out!" Malark celebrated. "We've actually done it..."

The fissure widened and Minister Jozlov, Garo, Ruslanova, Mashnaya, and Kosha squeezed through the opening. They stood up, stumbling, and wondering if everything was real.

"Where are we going?" asked Jozlov sensibly.

Kosha spat out dirt. "All this talk of atoms, molecules, tables, and chairs," he said as he felt the earth with his booted feet. "It's never literally true!"

"Cut the mustard," said Garo as she picked her nose.

Assuming command, Malark pointed into the far distance. "We make for the black forest. Doubtless, other people have failed, but we're going to succeed."

"Agreed," said Kosha as he observed Ruslanova watching the sunset.

Jozlov looked around her surroundings. "There's nothing...*dangerous* out here?"

"When Ulysses was trapped by Polyphemus the Cyclops he told the Cyclops that his name was Outis—which means Nobody," Ruslanova seemed to speak into the sunlight. "He poked Polyphemus in the eye and that was how he escaped. Then Polyphemus told the other cyclopes what had happened. When they asked him who had poked his eye, he said, *Nobody*—and they all laughed and called him crazy..."

"The wasteland is too small for nothing to be here," decided Malark.

"There will be nothing when I die," said Jozlov.

"It's going to be a long walk. We might as well start."

The runaway group started walking. Kosha cleared his throat as he laughed to himself.

"Why do you say there'll be nothing when you die?" he asked the minister. "We could say the same about being alive. Why is it something when we're alive and then nothing when we're dead? It may be the other way round…pass me that flask…"

Passing her flask of milk, Ruslanova returned to watching the sunset.

"Ah! The open air!" he chortled. "If there's no mystery to life then everything is solved; or not worth investigating. We know that isn't true. There are many abysses in books; many more in classrooms; I've concluded that everything and something confuses me." He returned the flask to its owner. "The wasteland is my toilet. That's *my* premonition."

Jozlov had stopped listening. She too stared at the sunset. "Look at that, Malark…"

"I only wanted to draw." He was slowing down. "We need the *Old Hall Manuscript*."

"A little sacred music never did anyone harm."

"Indeed."

Her eyeline grazed his ankles and then slowly lifted to his face. "You agree with me?"

"Yes…"

Their thinning bodies munched every last morsel of energy, and they swayed their arms like bumptious clergymen sniffing for God. In the night sky, there appeared a trail of smoke.

DAY FOUR

"...You will never reform me!" shouted the prisoner next door for the second time. The voice rang out every couple of minutes. It was dark and cold in the dream.

Fibber woke up next to Yulia who was wearing his trousers as a blanket. Staggering onto his feet, Fibber surveyed the bilious ceiling of the circus tent. He clomped outside where he ran around the circus tent for several minutes. His feet made hollow booms and he soon tired and stopped by the entrance. He sat cross-legged on the ground where he fell backwards and held his arms above his head. "I'm still drunk," he insisted. He got to his feet and swaggered to the covered wagon. The door was open and the Strongman's arm was hanging out of the entrance. The sleeping hand held a half-empty tankard that Fibber pried away and drank from.

"These bloody ancients must excuse my manners that so neglected you," quoted Fibber.

Draining the remaining froth, Fibber stood unsatisfied. His stomach was cavernous and not unlike the humid excess of the fourth floor herself. Gazing inside the wagon, Fibber found the Strongman sleeping on the floorboards. The Astrologer and the Maestro were sleeping nearby in vulgar positions on the sides. Honza's feet dangled from his bunk-ish compartment and the Bearded Lady's feet poked out of a barrel.

"He *was* pickled—but this is ridiculous," chortled Fibber as he crept inside the wagon. He sat next to the Maestro's scruffy head, picked up a glass of absinthe, and poured it over him.

"Oh God—!"

"Pay careful consideration to the bishop if you want God to consider you," Fibber said.

"Overseer," replied the Maestro as he clawed his lips, "we made too much merry."

"I should have gone to bed. But I've been told that I should never neglect a widow." He dabbed absinthe on the Maestro's head. "Those widows downstairs are the *most* neglectful."

The Maestro's throat was razor-sharp. "You are about as holy as concrete if judgement begins and ends with holiness."

"If concrete were free you would try to sell it." He spat on the Maestro's face.

A delicate moan came from the floor. "I can't feel my face," the Strongman gargled.

"If you don't know the time then I have some imagination to spare," laughed Fibber.

"Everything is a matter of time," the Maestro stuttered as he got up. Rubbing his forehead in the semi-darkness of the covered wagon a certain anxiety grabbed him. "The time?"

Fibber shrugged as though he had received nothing in the post. "It's nine."

The Maestro shot up and his head collided with Honza's feet which spasmed. "All of you!" He was gasping and puffing like a dragon. "We have an hour to get ready. Get up!"

"You got a brain like a sieve," said Honza. His feet twitched in existential agitation.

"When did you wake up?" asked the Maestro.

"I couldn't sleep! I'm terrified because of you—*you jackass*! I've got to go out there and replace my food with verbs!"

Fibber arose in the cramped, half-dark space where limbs bespeckled the theatrical interior. He yawned and then recited loudly,

> The play you must venture now
> Drain lines from poetic cow
> Without warning on you plough
> Play *Othello*, take thine vow
> The muse returns, brows he burns
> And once sold there are no returns.

Honza poked his eyes over the side. He watched the Overseer for a long time. "Dumb." Suddenly, the Strongman laughed awake. The Astrologer pulled hair out of her mouth. "What's so funny?" The wagon unbalanced when the Strongman creaked up. "Diogenes kept his belongings in a jar. That's why all my lines are in my noggin!"

There followed the unbuttoning of clothing after which togas were tightened, lines recited and drips of alcoholic sweat dribbled down everybody's foreheads. The combined locomotion of the Metaphysical Circus forced Fibber out of the wagon where he practically fell onto the ground. When he stood back up Angeloff, Drast, and Pommel grabbed their guitars and started tuning them as the habited prophet, Angeloff, applied his toga with great precision.

"The Bluebloods want to destroy any moral challenge to the established social morality," Angeloff told Fibber. "What will moral relativists think when I forget my lines?"

"What makes the lines right is that they are *learned*," Drast interjected academically.

"It's for that reason that you will never understand *Despotism's Isle*," sighed Pommel. "The law of gravity doesn't apply to your arrogance because God has a sense of humour."

"Gentlemen, please!" Angeloff yawned. "We need to shield our eyes from the naked lady because God hates those."

Yulia stood in front of the circus tent. Drast and Pommel dropped their guitars onto their feet, reached down to comfort their soles, whacked their heads together, and collapsed.

Fibber strutted over to Yulia. "Who are you? Some many-breasted fertility goddess?"

"Does two count?"

"Sunday Mass." He winked and laughed. "Would you be a neglectful widow if I died?"

"Making light of the world's cruelties is the lowest form of thought."

"I admit the question was half-formed," he replied. "But do you have an answer?"

The unhealthy sound of the wagon's wheels cranking as everyone poured out was punctuated by the crackling of dry bread torn, dipped in last night's tankards, and consumed.

The Strongman, the Astrologer, the Maestro, and Honza were dazzled by anxiety as they stumbled around eating nodules of bread and wetting scorched tongues with ale remains.

Searching for his script Angeloff suddenly stopped. "Where is Desdemona?"

"The aliens took him. I have their number," replied Fibber as he clapped his hands. "Karl Muck had the same problem because he was German."

"The Bearded Lady is neither Swedish, Russian, English, nor Lithuanian," listed off the Maestro as though he hated those nationalities the most.

"Tell that to the police," said the Astrologer.

Drast strummed a major chord, "Fibber is the police! He is the Overseer!"

"Self-appointed," came the unimpressed reply. Her stomach rumbled.

"Self-evident, actually," said Fibber as he kicked Angeloff's behind. Standing up the prophet climbed onstage and watched as the other performers followed and started rehearsing.

As they sprinted through a performance of Act One, the Maestro un-pocketed a miniature portrait of his mother. She was a fierce woman who was wearing a golden robe, a sheathed broadsword, and poorly sewn sandals. There was, regrettably, a sign behind her that said: "Mental Ward".

The Maestro sighed, pocketed the miniature, and watched the play through his fingers.

"Tush, never tell me," recited Drast, "I take it much unkindly that thou, Iago, who has had my purse, as if the strings were thine, shouldn't know of this."

"S'blood," replied Angeloff with vigour. "But you will not hear me. If ever I did dream of such a matter, abhor me."

"Thou told'st me, thou did'st hold him in thy hate!"

Pommel, meanwhile, poked the Maestro with his guitar. "He's talking about Othello."

"I know that—you *gobshite*," replied the Maestro. "I was remembering why I entered this discipline—instead of counting beans somewhere."

"Ah…"

To the right of the tottering stage, Fibber wrapped a blanket around Yulia.

He enjoyed making her warm but there was, simultaneously, a strange seriousness about it all. "Everyone will be typing downstairs and then they have to come and watch this."

"Do you mean we're watching the culmination of something?"

He gently rubbed her arms. "I'm not sure."

"It's as if Bruno Giordino were a gestalt and came to shock the people of the Tectum by saying that God was infinite because she was the manifestation of an infinite universe."

"Plagiarist."

"What does stealing from Agrippa and Ficino prove? That the Renaissance was predicated upon theft—and you have to steal a few ideas if you want to have a Renaissance."

"There's an exit hatch to the roof," Fibber said suddenly. He was serious and very sober. "I know these things. Will you come with me?"

She turned to look at him, frowned at what she found, and swallowed. "Up there?"

"If these typewriters produce the worst performance of *Othello* but nothing else then I will have been worrying in vain...if the play is meant to distract us, however...we need to get out of here...before things get ugly." He looked very grave. "I spoke to Kosha about this."

"You stole an idea."

"Only a worry...but offers and worries are the same thing." He paused and stared. "Keep my offer in mind. All right?" There was no humour in his eyes as he exhaled safely.

The runaway group woke up in a depression in the wasteland. First Malark awoke and then he poked Minister Jozlov, Garo, Ruslanova, Mashnaya, and Kosha. Like a small cave, the depression peered out onto the wasteland that stretched for miles into the distance. The expedition suffered through a breakfast of milk and biscuits and then started walking.

They had been stumbling for three hours when Mashnaya ran slowly up to Malark. "You're a painter...have you ever heard of colour music?"

"It sounds overrated." He avoided breaking his ankle for the fourth time.

"It's music visualized using colours...the most successful colour music was *Fantasia* where *Toccata and Fugue in D Minor* was accompanied by crazy patterns on the screen."

"Can you be an authority on folk music? That's what I want to know," said Malark. The wasteland stretched into the distance everywhere they looked. It was flat and furry, like walking through the knee-length equivalent of coconut hair. Bumps came and went like muddy puddles and no birds were singing because there were no trees for them to live in.

"Milk and biscuits…*half* a biscuit…for the past nine miles that's all we have eaten," mumbled Minister Jozlov. "How do you live like this?"

"Salaries are weapons…if you die, minister, Charun shall finish you off with one blow from his mighty hammer," replied Kosha.

"I joined the civil service because I never liked people talking. You should have been there when I showed my sister a cease-and-desist letter." Her eyes traced the land. "*A pig!*"

The rest of the group watched Minister Jozlov peel off to the right and hold on to her ministerial wimple as she ran desperately through knee-length shrubs and crude patches of tall brown grass.

"Each person is an end in themselves," said Kosha. "Go on, minister, you sad creature: chase those imaginary piggies. I won't be adopting any moral legislation that *you* produce."

"She's not joking!" interrupted Garo who pointed her finger. "A pig—over there!"

"Get out of my way," grunted Kosha as he pushed Garo and Mashnaya out of his way. He hobbled through shrubs and undergrowth, licking his lips as he approached the pig.

Malark watched in despair. "Get back! That thing will take your hand off!"

"Come here piggy." Jozlov imagined the critter dappled with apple sauce and rosemary. "I promise I won't blow your house down…"

"You're hoping that a matriarchy is going to materialize," said Kosha as he drooled. "But matriarchal societies are open-minded as well as promiscuous. Think of all those babies!"

Stopping suddenly, Jozlov screamed, threw up her arms, and started running in the opposite direction. Watching her fly past, Kosha raised his eyebrows. "Don't scare it!"

"It's got an arm!" she screamed as she pointed to the human hand in its mouth. Then Kosha screamed like a seal pup and held onto his goggles as he quickly overtook the minister.

Malark laughed loudly.

Mashnaya and Ruslanova debated whether folk-music-experts were logical impossibilities. They decided to postpone their conclusion for another day.

Embracing one another, Jozlov and Kosha kissed each other on the cheek. "I'm sorry that I made fun of you," Kosha said.

"We shall live to fight another day," replied Jozlov. Amid their embrace, Kosha's hands reached her behind. Slapping his hands away, Jozlov retrieved her body from his embrace and found an appropriate lump of moss on which to stand. "Life continues."

Scrambling through shrubs and ferns Malark tripped, fell over, and got up again. "Where did that hog come from? There must be a farm here or something!"

"Impossible. Farm on the moon and you'd have better crops," replied Ruslanova. "There are some Australian tribes who say that the moon created the first couple."

Kosha sighed romantically, "Where *are* Adam and Eve when you need them?"

The trail of smoke they had followed after leaving the Tectum was lower than usual. It hung in the sky like a sable string and flitted restlessly across the half-windy horizon. Garo, tensing her huge calves, could see a building about a mile away. Jumping through puddles and sun-eaten shrubs she made her way towards the building: a burning farm-stead. The others followed Garo, coughing lightly as smoke from the incendiary structure tickled their throats and lungs. They could see a log cabin, a wooden shed, and a chicken pen.

Nearby was a ditch where a burning rover had either crashed or been left to smoulder. Its two passengers were charred beyond recognition. Pigs were wandering every-where, and forlorn chickens pecked the hot mud that sizzled their beaks and sent them squawking.

The sight drove Garo to desperation. "Once upon a time, they would have been our saviours. We can't go to the black forest. We might as well go to the moon!" she exclaimed.

"If we abstain from drinking and carry our knives then we'll make it to Fairyland. Would you like that, Ruslanova?"

Ruslanova slapped her. "Pull yourself together! Shall we beat those cyclopes?"

"Too much violence," protested Garo. "It doesn't change anything—"

Pushing Ruslanova out of his way, Malark then took hold of Garo: "Damn you," he said as Ruslanova waited to see if his interrogation would outperform hers. "Violence doesn't change anything? It destroyed this farm and the people who lived here." He turned around. "What is more, minister, if you knew anything about this—I'll have that blue hide of yours!"

Massaging her temples and staggering behind the charred remains of the chicken pen, Minister Jozlov mumbled to herself and then to the sad runaway group that she had joined.

"I don't...I'm as ignorant as you are...every bit as rejected as every person here," she said as she recoiled at the sight of singed perches. "Those quill-pushers gave me a one-way ticket to stone heads, mountains of paperwork, and certain death."

Move by her performance, Malark offered a hopeless laugh. "We're going to be famous! With you as my model, my work will be everywhere. The artist is defined by his subject."

"But you blackmailed me!"

"It was productive blackmail. I don't have to tell you how rarely blackmail works." Itching his sides, he looked around the dead farm. "Maybe art is nothing; or something real."

Ruslanova ignored her empty stomach, sat cross-legged, and counted her fingers. "Business interests are a part of society. If they destroy society then they destroy themselves."

Caught in a cloud of smoke, Mashnaya prowled the super-heated mud towards Kosha. "Do you have any ideas?"

Kosha wrenched off his goggles, kissed them, and then tossed them onto the fire. "These people were important enough to be murdered. If they knew something, perhaps, then they would have had to be taught that three people can keep a secret if two of them are dead."

"We must be stupid and not know anything," concluded Mashnaya as he frowned.

"We all matter, Mashnaya—and remember logic. We need logic now more than ever." He enjoyed the heat because it reminded him of the furnace. "The mysteries of the Father, the Son, and the Holy Spirit are beyond comprehension. If we use logic, however, I can be three people simultaneously, without compromising that unity, and able to show this."

Malark abandoned Garo who had long since given up. He stepped noiselessly towards Kosha who was smiling sadly to himself. "I can't believe—you just proved that you're God," said Malark as he slapped his arms by his sides. "I've slogged through the past three days like nobody's business and you decide that now is the best time for you to reveal your divinity? What happened? Did the burning corpses bring you out of your stupor and back to humanity?"

"I'm not God. But if God exists, he'll show up shortly," replied Kosha firmly.

There came from the distance the sound of rumbling. It started as something fake and gradually became organic and omnipresent. There were people and machines on the horizon, spread across like matchsticks. Heading for the runaway group, the matchsticks thickened and grew louder and sharper. The first person to recognize the mass of machinery and people was Garo. She walked towards the rumbling. "Holy crap," she muttered.

In the meantime, the fourth floor was filling up with people who scrambled inside and who were directed by the Maestro whose eyes were widening at the amount of money he wasn't making. The audience members held typewriters like new-borns, dirtying the room with their unwashed skin and clothing.

"Citizens!" announced the Maestro. "I pray that you enjoy *The Tragedy of Othello*."

When a woman caught his attention, he waved her down. "Madam—?"

"I must…keep typing," said Novikoff. Holding her typewriter like a massive calculator, she was typing words and grinding her teeth when mistakes were made.

"Madam," parlayed the Maestro as he flexed his rigid fingers, "the typewriter will exist when the play concludes."

"I can't concentrate," she said as she stared down her nose, "when your fingers touch mine!"

"You are steering towards the Isle of Rhodes," he warned. "Give me the typewriter—"

When he tried to pry the typewriter away from her, she screamed, "No! No! No!"

The crowd around her was jolted and their distracted red eyes targeted the Maestro who capitulated and allowed Novikoff, her typewriter and her stockpiled paranoia to pass. Moving away nervously, the Maestro tripped on a child and then apologized to the girl's mother.

"Why are we watching *Othello* on a Sunday?" The mother wore a shawl and tattered socks. She held onto her daughter as she typed with the other hand. "Is that blasphemy?"

The back of the stage had been partitioned using a medical curtain from Doctor Grinko. Due to a stomach ulcer, he was unable to attend.

"Boss!" hissed the Strongman. "Come here!"

The Maestro popped his head around the corner. "What do you want, *Cassio*?"

Grabbing his toga from the ground, the Strongman rushed over to the Maestro. "I forgot about the circus tent— we should have built the stage inside," he admitted.

"Your only job was to build the stage inside the circus tent—and if geometry is as consistent as arithmetic, then you are built for dumbassery."

"Architecture is a brand of truth. It dreams of its own accord." The Strongman returned backstage where Honza memorized his lines by praying them.

"Had it pleas'd heaven to pickle me with affliction, had they buttered all kinds of sores and shames on my bare head…cucumbered me in poverty to the very lips, sausaged to captivity me and my utmost hopes…" He flicked through his script and resigned himself to mediocrity.

Proximate to the culinary Othello, the two musicians were hiding under a blanket sewn from used brown paper bags. Drast and Pommel wished that they could eat their guitars.

Meanwhile, Angeloff prayed the hunger away. "Iago cannot be *that* evil," he chuntered as he shaved in the mirror and kicked the ale-filled basin at his feet. "He doesn't even have an ideology..."

"What do you think is wrong with these typewriter people?" asked Drast.

"Why do you promptly assume the negative?" replied Angeloff. "Why pump an authoritarian atmosphere into an already smelly one? Do you think that describing a child as *bright* means that we have used the word in a non-technical way?"

Honza took a deep breath. He stood up on a stool. "I should have pomegranate in some place of my soul a drop of patience. But, alas, to milkshake me a fixed figure for the time of scorn to gnocchi his slow unmoving finger at. Yet could I goulash that too, well, very well..."

The brown paper bag blanket scratched the underside of Pommel's chin. "It may be a developmental sequence of behaviours." He ignored the vertically challenged Othello. "An interpretation of memorized stimuli?"

Drying his face, Angeloff scoffed. "Don't think too hard about divinity. You'll make your head hurt. You would do well to remember the word holistic: we ought to focus on these people and their typewriters as a whole, as opposed to thinking of them as individual components."

Raising his clawed hand and straining his neck muscles, Honza removed his socks. "But there...where I have jerk-chickened my heart...where I must calamari or lobster no life... the fountain from which my current eggplants, or else noodled up, to be noodled thence...or milk it as a cistern for foul toads to kebab and cupcake in!" He pointed to the ale-stained Bearded Lady who had recited the word stereo-type for the thousandth time. "Cheese-stuffed-jalapenos thy complexion there…patience, thou young and rose-lipp'd cherubin, aye, there, look grim as hell—"

"I'll see you on the other side," replied the Bearded Lady as he coughed up blood.

Drast slapped his forehead. "I think I've cracked this thing about God. Have you ever heard of the Mignon Delusion? It's where someone fantasizes that their biological parents are imposters and that their *real* parents are celebrities who are going to zoom in and rescue them. The fact remains that we're the children of God. But we've been lumpen with mortal parents who tell us to brush our fucking teeth."

Honza got down from the stool. He turned and sucked his teeth. "Drast, do you remember that time you said something I didn't care about?" He paused. "That's right now."

"Break a leg. Maybe I can break it for you?"

"I'm busy. Can I ignore you another time?"

Unbeknownst to the members of the Metaphysical-Circus-cum-The-King's-Men, Fibber was searching behind the circus tent for the exit hatch and discovered the aperture's outline. Testing the opening device that consisted of a hidden button on the reverse side of a brick, he was satisfied with the mechanics and subsequently returned to the barking typewriting crowd.

Time was of the essence, and Fibber accepted that he had chosen action over typing. Now that he was on the verge of survival, however, he started wondering what was beyond it.

He returned to Yulia on the edge of the crowd. "My offer stands…we're ready to go."

"We can't stay and watch some?" asked Yulia, knowing that the crowd might see through them.

"But you've already seen it?" He was terrified.

"They've made improvements. A change for the better wouldn't be worse." She smiled. "My caring for others is a step in the right direction."

Biting his nails Fibber watched the stage. He worried that the crowd would revolt. He doubted that they would accept anything less than excellence.

Fibber stood behind Yulia. He tightened the straps on his boots. He sighed as though he were about to recite poetry to a business conference of malicious Blueblood minds.

On the brink of their past destruction, the peasant army noticed a group of people by the farmstead. Staring through his telescope, Captain Gurkin grew impatient and scowled in displeasure. He lowered his telescope when he heard a galloping horse. "Captain, do we engage?" asked the Student on horseback. Tall shrubberies of gun barrels paraded behind Gurkin's head as he made up his mind. "They are Plum Lukum's scout patrol," he replied. They will be hanged, drawn, and quartered like the foreign bilge they are. You are an imaginative woman, sergeant—dispatch the rifle squad."

"Captain, with all due respect," clanking boots backgrounded her words, "if Plum Lukum travelled through the eastern channel, then how—?"

"Are you questioning orders?" A venomous excretion was emitted from the raid tank. "Exterminate them!"

Below the raid tank, peasant soldiers wearing makeshift armour wandered tiredly. Snowing lightly the cold weather shadowed the rifle squad that chimed onto a horse-drawn wagon. In a matter of minutes, the wagon was speeding towards the farmstead's new owners.

Viewing the oncoming wagon with complete abandon Kosha raised his arms. "I walk towards Zeno of Elea; towards contradictory conclusions; towards that which is both limited and unlimited. There are as many good men as there are which exist—I walk towards them."

The wagon stopped a hundred metres away as Kosha stepped through the snow.

The rifle squad clanked off of the wagon and doddered in the direction of Kosha. They held their loaded barrels horizontally and moved noisily through the crunching snow and frost.

"They will kill you!" shouted Ruslanova. "You must come back!"

Malark held her back. "He is going to meet the responsible one."

"I walk in the direction of evil men who must be insignificant...but who are unlimited in their evil," prayed Kosha as the barrels surrounded him. "We shall see who wins. We shall see contradictions in bloom...*because all is mind.*"

"Fire!" ordered the Student.

The snowy geysers traced a line to his chest where four pockets unzipped. Stunned for several moments Kosha subsequently fell backwards.

Seeing this, Malark ran towards the chicken pen where he was gunned down. The body of the deputy overseer made contact with the hot ground.

Ruslanova made for the cabin but her back was unzipped by seven cartridges. She was dead in moments after falling onto the charred grass.

Garo was successful in avoiding the bullets but was, regrettably, crushed when the roof of the shed collapsed on top of her.

Mashnaya was the only one who ran away, towards the black forest, presumably. But one cartridge entered his back whilst another shattered his right knee. He collapsed into a shrub where he bled to death.

The last to die was Minister Jozlov who suffered a heart attack but who was half-alive when they shot her in the head.

As they inspected their handiwork the rifle squad rifled through pockets of the dead. "This one has milk," one soldier said. He was wearing a cooking pot for a helmet, red hiking boots, and two bracelets strung together from the bleached bones of rodents.

"A bony ass," said another. Her hair was short and brown and she had bruises all over her face from repeated beatings dispensed by a dead man. She nibbled Garo's last biscuit.

"You will return to formation," ordered the Student.

The rifle squad climbed aboard the horse-drawn wagon and returned to the army that now targeted a giant, stone silhouette on the horizon...

A hypocrisy of sound defined the fourth floor where the performance of *Othello* was undermined by hundreds of audience members pounding their typewriters. Fibber retreated from his senses, watching the play from the corner of his eye, preparing himself for the worst.

At some point, Yulia tugged his sleeve. "Do you hear that?" she whispered as fingers retracted from keys and the typewriters silenced throughout the room. "They're stopping."

All around them, dead eyes watched the stage as the play progressed, the actors casually ignoring the strange behaviour of their unwashed and intellectually stunted audience.

To his astonishment, Angeloff said a line at the same time an audience member did: "*How poor are they that have not patience!*"

Angeloff stopped. He identified the speaker in the front row.

"Or would you rather we stopped?" asked Angeloff.

"I know what happens," replied Novikoff below him. There was a grey man called Belinsky who was wearing a beige overcoat and shabby linen trousers. "We are all in agreement with her," he supported her and scoffed. "We have finished the play. We know what happens."

Yulia was surprised when she heard Oksana, her fellow prostitute, say, "I have Act Four. What about you?"

Every person in the huge crowd raised their hands simultaneously. "I have typed and stacked every act," Belinsky claimed as he flung his overcoat on the ground. Observing the manuscripts around him, Fibber believed that something terrible had started. He bided his time. Novikoff lifted her manuscript into the air, threw it on the ground, and propped her boot on it. "Me too," she said. "I have dog-eared the best parts and numbered the pages."

The tone of the crowd quickly changed from jubilation to despair. Tired gazes turned sour and hands were thrown up as manuscripts were kicked around the room by impatient feet.

"What the fuck does it mean?" moaned Belinsky.

"Was Shakespeare drunk?" asked another man whose nose was bright pink and shiny. He ripped his shirt open and poked his tumorous belly. "I've got more guts than Shakespeare!"

"What does it matter if charity is the reprieve of death?" asked Belinsky.

"I suggest that we *both* wrote it. You and I and each one of us has written this," said Oksana. "I don't understand why Othello believes him."

"Who, Iago?"

"That's just my point, Belinsky! Othello must realize that Iago will not be happy when he promotes Cassio. He must understand that Iago won't take that lying down! Then again maybe Othello has a developmental disorder: trust be the kindness that kills you in the end."

"This is the suspension of disbelief," argued Belinsky. "Without the suspension of disbelief, the mechanics of playwriting dissolve into dust. We would join a Roman cohort and storm the stage daily demanding justice for Desdemona—"

There was a child next to him who jumped up. He was bland and pasty looking. "Othello is gayer than Oscar Wilde," he declared to equal rapturous applause and disapproval. "He wouldn't mind giving his manservants a good lesson—if you know what I mean?"

"I'm homosexual and I *resent* that," Belinsky replied as he wagged his sallow finger. "I wrote the complete works of Oscar Wilde last night and I'm telling you that that guy is straighter than a man who's yanked his underwear to full capacity." He unzipped his trousers. "If you give me half a chance then I will volley my plastic warhead!"

The performers onstage watched these exchanges with disinterest.

Honza scurried to the front where he shouted: "If you all wrote the goddamn play then what's Roderigo's second line in Act Five, Scene One?"

The fourth floor rumbled like a well-attended church when the audience replied: "*I have no great devotion to the deed and yet he hath given me satisfying reasons!*"

"You got so many gaps in your skull it looks like your brain's in jail." The vertically challenged Othello stomped his feet, flicked his middle fingers, and stuck out his pink tongue. "I'm trying to work around culinary objects and you come along and know the play verbatim!"

"We're behind the Tectum's eyes; where the brain should be," preached Novikoff.

Oksana stood up and then pointed around the room. "We have become brains. We should take hold of the Tectum and touch it," was her plan and the people around her approved. "We shall see that the Tectum is no bodiless phantom. By tonight we will all despise death."

Belinsky quieted the crowd by appealing to the players. "Can we finish the play?" he asked as several hundred angry eyes turned their way. "What happens to Othello's brother?"

Honza practically exploded. "I'm Othello, you cretin!"

During this exchange, the Bearded Lady plotted behind the medical curtain. He concluded that the writers needed to be punished. He ran onstage where he called for action. "Do we all agree that Desdemona is a stereotype?"

"Yes!" replied the audience.

"We must burn every copy of *Othello*. We must teach Shakespeare that wrongs do not go unpunished. It will be as though he never existed. Who will join me?"

Belinsky and Oksana raised their hands as Novikoff encouraged others to do the same. Then scurrilous waves of hands battling their own stiff digits shot into the air.

Fibber and Yulia watched in horror as the raised hands gave way to shouts of hatred. "Burn the stupid thing!" said a woman wearing half a suit of armour and chewing tobacco.

"Time to jump ship when people burn books," muttered Yulia. "Show me the hatch."

"You will come?" Fibber was caught by his own exasperated frame of mind.

"Why are you standing there?"

The angry horde stacked manuscripts and doused them in liquor. The stacks were set alight when smokers pushed their way through the crowd and decided to turn up the heat.

"Let's get the hell out of here," advised Yulia. Fibber took her hand and guided her behind the circus tent where they avoided destruction.

The shape of Captain Gurkin's hand silhouetted against the sky halted the clanking soldiers. The Tectum was surrounded by men and women holding rifles, swords, and spears. Joining them were soldiers who emptied out of carts and wagons, their knives and semi-automatic weapons held against the sky. Captain Gurkin spoke briefly after rallying the soldiers with bursts of machine gun fire. "Who knew Plum Lukum could build invisible bases?"

The army's makeshift armour rattled as peasants laughed and raised their weapons.

"We know that Poseidon rode a magic chariot across the sea...but we have such a chariot within our hearts...our chariots shall ride across the toughest terrain!"

The army cheered relentlessly.

"Your orders are to exterminate the bilge! On the inside, kill everything!"

Loading their rifles with ceremonial copper bullets, the soldiers joined those with swords and spears and advanced on the Tectum.

After disembarking from the horse-drawn wagon, the Drinker followed the Gambler who struggled to carry a mortar launcher. The Gambler was wearing the remains of a three-piece suit that he had purchased fifteen years ago in the parliamentary district. He had straddled the storms of high society and had finished up penniless, homeless, and without influence. His face was mangled from beatings suffered at the hands of furious debtors. His nose was crooked and his eyes peered out from under a flattened pillow-like brow that badly blurred his vision. "Take a look at that thing," he said as they were swiftly caught in the Tectum's girthy shadow.

They trampled high grass and stepped in puddles of ooze.

"Hephaestus was the God of Fire but he was ugly and they chucked him off the damn mountain. Do you think he landed in that stone head?"

The Drinker pretended to agree as he secured a fresh bottle of whiskey from a child. "The other version of that story, where he complained that Zeus was abusing his mother," recalled the Drinker. "I find more believable."

"What in the name of Zeus does that mean? Why are we marching so slowly?" complained the Gambler.

"Jesus Christ agreed to the crucifixion," whispered the Drinker, "because there was no other way for him to prove the divine promise that he made to our ancestors."

A little girl covered in mortar rounds was confronted by the Gambler. She was shivering because she was up to her small ankles in a puddle of snow-laden mud. Patting her on the head, the Gambler removed several rounds from the girl's chest and then yanked her out of the mud.

The Drinker choked. "What do you think you're doing? The Holy Bible of weapons!"

"Feel free to blow your own legs off. But we've got to open that bulkhead."

Behind them, an old man wearing little more than a thin cloth-coloured sack was swinging a shovel around his head because he thought that demons were flying around him. "I have the biggest cataracts!" he declared as his shovel knocked out a malnourished teenager.

Squelching through mud, the Gambler was carrying his mortar launcher and eventually positioned his device on one of the sturdier square feet of grassy earth. He picked up one of the mortar rounds, kissed it goodbye, and then slipped it down the launching tube. He quickly covered his ears as the round caterwauled through the chilly morning air towards the bulkhead.

An explosion screamed and then dust rallied the encroaching mob who sneezed. Other peasants with mortar-launchers replicated the effort and the Tectum was subsequently bombarded from all directions.

Chunks of concrete crashed to the ground and the snow was covered by dust.

One side of the bulkhead whined off of its hinges and collapsed into the mud. It was then that the peasant army could see people scrambling for cover inside, on the first floor.

The Student galloped in the direction of the mouth of the Tectum. She galloped past armoured squads wearing clanging boots, spear-carrying alcoholics, and deranged children...

There were those inside the Tectum whose minds could not stretch to typewriters, let alone dramatic interpretations of Jacobean plays.

On the first floor, several moments earlier, simple folk had wandered amongst the chains wondering when their family members would return from the frivolities on the fourth.

Suddenly the bulkhead exploded, spraying metal, concrete, and cakes of bodies. Those who weren't killed in the explosion were dazed and stumbled back to their feet as armed civilians stormed the first floor and started slaughtering them. The mentally challenged squealed as their bodies were swamped with bad attitudes, bullets, and sharpened objects. Anatomies piled high as soldiers re-loaded their weapons and they ascended the staircase to the second floor where the occasional bystander was either shot or stabbed and left on the staircase.

They targeted the brothel and levelled a mortar round at the door, which sent splinters everywhere as peasant mercenaries stormed the brothel where they picked off the simpler prostitutes and clients who had stayed behind in the hope of avoiding their least favourite play.

Ignoring the massacre around him, Levitsky took a deep breath and started singing:

Plum Lukuuuuuum!
Sweet death, what is your tune?

A bullet entered Levitsky's forehead and the force of the impact whisked him to the ground. The man who had shot him was the Drinker. Inebriated and out of breath, he mourned his actions and then stared hopelessly around him.

"I have found a lifetime's supply of pistachios," the Gambler said as he strutted by carrying bags in his hands. "Want some?"

The Drinker gagged. "This isn't war—this is *murder*."

"What's the difference? We will give these toads more copper than they can handle," the Gambler laughed as he buttoned up his three-piece suit and exited the brothel gaily.

The soldiers ascended the staircase to the third floor where the mentally challenged children of the rich and the wealthy were murdered.

The wealth on the third floor pleased the soldiers who devoured family coffers and dressed themselves in jewels and rings. The dead eyes of Doctor Grinko watched moneyed peasants stepping over his corpse, the floor stained by the blood of butchered pets. Abandoned infants were thrown onto spears and then flung onto the knolls of the dead. The Gambler disembowelled cabinets that were rich in useless things. He tore out gold and silver from under green felt and then pocketed the less-damaged articles and imagined pawning them.

"Maybe if we croak these bastards we'll fix the country," he noted in passing as bodies burned.

"These illegal Belgian things corrupt the minds of the young."

Beside him was a soldier wearing thick glasses, furry knee-length boots, and necklaces. He was playing with the deceased Doctor Grinko's stethoscope. "There a doctor in the house?"

Packs of soldiers carrying books dropped them onto ever-expanding piles that were doused in liquor and set on fire.

The Student was rifling through someone's belongings when she found a copy of *The Relaxed Frog* by Dante Fibber. She pocketed the book of poetry, picked up the other books, and carried them to the nearest bonfire where she dumped them onto the flames.

The Gambler eyed her suspiciously and then kicked Grinko's body.

The Drinker found a bottle of absinthe to drink his sorrows away...

On the steps that led up to the fourth floor, the Chicken Boy was busying himself reading *Faust*. He lowered his book when he heard the thumping of boots against the staircase. "I knew they would come...the formal cause of this place is prison-related...its material cause is concrete...its efficient cause is the Blueblood Government...its final cause is marching up the stairs and they have a final solution in mind," he muttered to himself as the weaponised peasants appeared around the corner of the staircase. Their armour screeched against the walls and their boots riddled the confined space with noise. The Chicken Boy watched as two gun barrels became eight gun barrels with the occasional spear sticking out from between them.

"If I am to die...then let my ghost be one with the old philosophers—BOGACK!"

Two cracks whipped the Chicken Boy's chest and sent him hurtling down the stairs. The soldiers counted his fingers out of curiosity and then clattered up the staircase. The doors to the fourth floor burst open. Gunning down young and old alike, the soldiers progressed. The infrequent type-writer sparked as swarms of wounded people found pockets of stopgap safety.

In no time at all the Astrologer was shot and her body fell onto the stage. The Strongman watched this happen with anguish and then suddenly lost his mind and attacked the soldiers. He jumped offstage where he attacked the Drinker who had shot the only person who had ever mattered to him. Raising the Drinker above his head the Strongman launched him onto the covered wagon that overturned from the force of the dead body and subsequently caught fire. The Gambler made an attempt to shoot the Strongman but the latter punched him and killed him too. Fighting an entire rifle squad by himself the Strongman tossed peasants here and there. He screamed with anguish and was finally shot down by two soldiers who had crept up behind him.

Honza dodged falling concrete and blistered bodies that blocked exit strategies with their dead slack weight. He crawled behind the circus tent where he searched for the aforementioned hatch which he had discovered the previous day when he had smoked a blunt.

He wondered if you needed a special key. Was the hatch only for repairs?

Kicking the wall in frustration the shape showed itself. He kicked again and crawled through the hatch. "Bring me the dwarf," shouted a beer-soaked monster behind him.

He was hyperventilating when he shut the hatch. Using his hands, he located the locking mechanism and decidedly locked the hatch.

It was dark.

He discovered a piece of heavy machinery. He shoved the thing in front of the hatch. Then opening a box of matches he swore quietly. He could never find any matches.

He wiped his forehead when something dripped on him. Touching a route away from the hatch, he discovered a spiral-like staircase that ascended into the ceiling.

He accepted that going down was overrated. He accepted that he would never go downstairs again and then assumed that it had to be better wherever the staircase led him…

The roof of the Tectum was tarred, flat, and frozen stiff by altitude and cold temperatures. It was windswept and eddies of freeze-packed snow swirled ceaselessly in small cold hurricanes. Fibber thought it was like a landing pad for a flying machine invented by an ancient civilization. His sense of scale was rocked and dwarfed as he clomped across the frozen featureless ocean. He reached a covered area that had been left by the migrant workers; except those who it had sheltered once upon a time were dead—whereas Fibber and Yulia commandeered the dark cavity, sat next to each other, and pulled a blanket over their kneecaps. "You must be cold," Fibber said as the wind blew and tossed detached frost around the roof.

She warmed her hands. "I had a dream last night."

"What of?"

"It was…something bad had happened."

"Continue," Fibber said when a tense giggle stopped his face.

"I was not sure what had happened…but the feeling was that it was…disastrous. We had both been selected to be placed into a pod." She paused for memory. "A space pod."

"A space pod?"

"Our clothes were taken away and we were placed in the pod. It was paraded down the street. We were on show." Her nose was frozen stiff. "Inside the pod, they played soothing music…except the music had no effect on my mood…it was as though I couldn't hear the music and I continued to be… afraid."

"What did you know with certainty?"

Yulia smiled. "That we were going to be launched into space. You were unconcerned when I told you that I was worried about our *being* launched into space. I told you to hold me but you didn't hear me." When she said this, she had to catch her breath and gather her memories. "We were finally launched into space and we rocketed up through the clouds before passing through the lithosphere. I shut my eyes through the whole voyage…"

"I didn't say anything?"

"I asked you if we had passed through the lithosphere. You replied that we had. But the whole time I felt unsafe— like something terrible would happen."

It was then that fresh snow descended from the sky. It coated everything, maintaining the freezing surface temperature.

"Were we going to another planet?" asked Fibber.

"No…we stayed…"

Looking out at the featureless ocean that comprised the roof and its cold components, Fibber nodded pleasantly and then took Yulia's hands into his and rubbed them to warm them.

"That's because we're the originals," Fibber said as he beamed like the Cheshire Cat. "There will never be anyone like us again. I'm the original Fibber. You're the original Yulia."

A hundred metres away the hatch clattered open. It was Honza and he spotted them.

"He's the original Honza," Fibber added as the dwarf shut the hatch behind him, found a discarded crate, and covered the hatch by pushing the crate over it.

Pleased with himself Honza locked his hands in his pockets. He half-ran over to Fibber and Yulia who were happy to see him safe and sound. They welcomed him under their blanket.

THE END

ACKNOWLEDGEMENTS

I want to thank Montag Press for publishing this novel. I also want to thank my wonderful editor Charlie Franco, and my great designer Rick Febre, for helping to publish this novel.

I want to thank Gabriel Chad Boyer for picking up grammar explosions in the final draft, and Connor De Bruler and Charis Emanon.

I also want to thank my Mum for keeping the fridge filled when I stayed with her, so that I could hack away at this manuscript in her lower apartment.

Lastly, I want to thank my partner, Ellie, for supporting an unemployed author with neuroses and dreams – which are probably the same thing.

AUTHOR BIO

Dr. Walker Zupp is a Bermudian author. He received his Ph.D. in Creative Writing from the University of Exeter. He currently lives in Cornwall, where he is a member of the Cornish Writers association, and the British Wittgenstein Society.

OTHER NOVELS BY WALKER ZUPP

Martha

"A freewheelingly scabrous, energetic, and darkly funny tale, pinpricked with pathos and sympathy, all concealing a strange sort of seriousness. Probably the strangest and most scatologically unbridled book you'll read this year, and that's a recommendation."

— George Green, author of *Hawk*

Nakadai

"One can picture Walker Zupp's sly grin as he composes Nakadai, an absurdist fantasy narrated by a grad student where a philosophical genius is empowered and enslaved by an inter-dimensional being called the Great Word who plots to invade the world. Written with breath-taking pace, language, academics, and eastern and western civilization are skewered by Zupp's rapier wit. Zupp captures the pathos and absurdity of contemporary life as his prose propels the reader into a parallel world that often feels eerily like our own."

— Stephen Scott Whitaker,
National Book Critics Circle

Printed in Great Britain
by Amazon